SANCTUARY

SANCTUARY

WILLIAM FAULKNER

VINTAGE BOOKS

A Division of Random House

NEW YORK

SANCTUARY

FROM BEYOND the screen of bushes which surrounded the spring, Popeye watched the man drinking. A faint path led from the road to the spring. Popeye watched the man—a tall, thin man, hatless, in worn gray flannel trousers and carrying a tweed coat over his arm—emerge from the path and kneel to drink from the spring.

The spring welled up at the root of a beech tree and flowed away upon a bottom of whorled and waved sand. It was surrounded by a thick growth of cane and brier, of cypress and gum in which broken sunlight lay sourceless. Somewhere, hidden and secret yet nearby, a bird sang three notes and ceased.

In the spring the drinking man leaned his face to the broken and myriad reflection of his own drinking. When he rose up he saw among them the shattered reflection of Popeye's straw hat, though he had heard no sound.

He saw, facing him across the spring, a man of under size, his hands in his coat pockets, a cigarette slanted side of his face squinted against the smoke like a mask carved into two simultaneous expressions.

From his hip pocket Popeye took a soiled handkerchief and spread it upon his heels. Then he squatted, facing the man across the spring. That was about four oclock on an afternoon in May. They squatted so, facing one another across the spring, for two hours. Now and then the bird sang back in the swamp, as though it were worked by a clock; twice more invisible automobiles passed along the highroad and died away. Again the bird sang.

"And of course you dont know the name of it," the man across the spring said. "I dont suppose you'd know a bird at all, without it was singing in a cage in a hotel lounge, or cost four dollars on a plate." Popeye said nothing. He squatted in his tight black suit, his right-hand coat pocket sagging compactly against his flank, twisting and pinching cigarettes in his little, doll-like hands, spitting into the spring. His skin had a dead, dark pallor. His nose was faintly aquiline, and he had no chin at all. His face just went away, like the face of a wax doll set too near a hot fire and forgotten. Across his vest ran a platinum chain like a spider web. "Look here," the other man said. "My name is Horace Benbow. I'm a lawyer in Kinston. I used to live in Jefferson yonder; I'm on my way there now. Anybody in this county can tell you I am harmless. If it's whiskey, I dont care how much you all make or sell or buy. I just stopped here for a drink of water. All I want to do is get to town, to Jefferson."

Popeye's eyes looked like rubber knobs, like they'd

"Why didn't we cut straight across up the hill?" Benbow said.

"Through all them trees?" Popeye said. His hat jerked in a dull, vicious gleam in the twilight as he looked down the hill where the jungle already lay like a lake of ink. "Jesus Christ."

It was almost dark. Popeye's gait had slowed. He walked now beside Benbow, and Benbow could see the continuous jerking of the hat from side to side as Popeye looked about with a sort of vicious cringing. The hat just reached Benbow's chin.

Then something, a shadow shaped with speed, stooped at them and on, leaving a rush of air upon their very faces, on a soundless feathering of taut wings, and Benbow felt Popeye's whole body spring against him and his hand clawing at his coat. "It's just an owl," Benbow said. "It's nothing but an owl." Then he said: "They call that Carolina wren a fishingbird. That's what it is. What I couldn't think of back there," with Popeye crouching against him, clawing at his pocket and hissing through his teeth like a cat. He smells black, Benbow thought; he smells like that black stuff that ran out of Bovary's mouth and down upon her bridal veil when they raised her head.

A moment later, above a black, jagged mass of trees, the house lifted its stark square bulk against the failing sky.

The house was a gutted ruin rising gaunt and stark out of a grove of unpruned cedar trees. It was a landmark, known as the Old Frenchman place, built before

"Professor," Popeye said. "He's got a book with him."

"What's he doing here?"

"I dont know. I never thought to ask. Maybe to read the book."

"He came here?"

"I found him at the spring."

"Was he trying to find this house?"

"I dont know," Popeye said. "I never thought to ask." The woman was still looking at him. "I'll send him on to Jefferson on the truck," Popeye said. "He said he wants to go there."

"Why tell me about it?" the woman said.

"You cook. He'll want to eat."

"Yes," the woman said. She turned back to the stove. "I cook. I cook for crimps and spungs and feebs. Yes. I cook."

In the door Popeye watched her, the cigarette curling across his face. His hands were in his pockets. "You can quit. I'll take you back to Memphis Sunday. You can go to hustling again." He watched her back. "You're getting fat here. Laying off in the country. I wont tell them on Manuel Street."

The woman turned, the fork in her hand. "You bastard," she said.

"Sure," Popeye said. "I wont tell them that Ruby Lamar is down in the country, wearing a pair of Lee Goodwin's throwed-away shoes, chopping her own firewood. No. I'll tell them Lee Goodwin is big rich."

"You bastard," the woman said. "You bastard."

"Sure," Popeye said. Then he turned his head. There was a shuffling sound across the porch, then a man

ii

WHEN THE WOMAN entered the dining-room, carrying a platter of meat, Popeye and the man who had fetched the jug from the kitchen and the stranger were already at a table made by nailing three rough planks to two trestles. Coming into the light of the lamp which sat on the table, her face was sullen, not old; her eyes were cold. Watching her, Benbow did not see her look once at him as she set the platter on the table and stood for a moment with that veiled look with which women make a final survey of a table, and went and stooped above an open packing case in a corner of the room and took from it another plate and knife and fork, which she brought to the table and set before Benbow with a kind of abrupt yet unhurried finality, her sleeve brushing his shoulder.

As she was doing that, Goodwin entered. He wore muddy overalls. He had a lean, weathered face, the jaws covered by a black stubble; his hair was gray at the temples. He was leading by the arm an old man with a long stood just inside the door, listening to them talking, listening to the stranger talking and to the thick, soft sound of the jug as they passed it among themselves. "That fool," the woman said. "What does he want. . . ." She listened to the stranger's voice; a quick, faintly outlandish voice, the voice of a man given to much talk and not much else. "Not to drinking, anyway," the woman said, quiet inside the door. "He better get on to where he's going, where his women folks can take care of him."

She listened to him. "From my window I could see the grape arbor, and in the winter I could see the hammock too. But in the winter it was just the hammock. That's why we know nature is a she; because of that conspiracy between female flesh and female season. So each spring I could watch the reaffirmation of the old ferment hiding the hammock; the green-snared promise of unease. What blossoms grapes have, this is. It's not much: a wild and waxlike bleeding less of bloom than leaf, hiding and hiding the hammock, until along in late May, in the twilight, her—Little Belle's—voice would be like the murmur of the wild grape itself. She never would say, 'Horace, this is Louis or Paul or Whoever' but 'It's just Horace.' Just, you see; in a little white dress in the twilight, the two of them all demure and quite alert and a little impatient. And I couldn't have felt any more foreign to her flesh if I had begot it myself.

"So this morning—no; that was four days ago; it was Thursday she got home from school and this is Tuesday—I said, 'Honey, if you found him on the train, he probably belongs to the railroad company. You cant take him from hind me, forgetting about the other one in which I could see her face, see her watching the back of my head with pure dissimulation. That's why nature is 'she' and Progress is 'he'; nature made the grape arbor, but Progress invented the mirror."

"He's crazy," the woman said inside the door, listening.

"But that wasn't quite it. I thought that maybe the spring, or maybe being forty-three years old, had upset me. I thought that maybe I would be all right if I just had a hill to lie on for a while— It was that country. Flat and rich and foul, so that the very winds seem to engender money out of it. Like you wouldn't be surprised to find that you could turn in the leaves off the trees, into the banks for cash. That Delta. Five thousand square miles, without any hill save the bumps of dirt the Indians made to stand on when the River overflowed.

"So I thought it was just a hill I wanted; it wasn't Little Belle that set me off. Do you know what it was?"

"He is," the woman said inside the door. "Lee ought not to let—"

Benbow had not waited for any answer. "It was a rag with rouge on it. I knew I would find it before I went into Belle's room. And there it was, stuffed behind the mirror: a handkerchief where she had wiped off the surplus paint when she dressed and stuck it behind the mantel. I put it into the clothes-bag and took my hat and walked out. I had got a lift on a truck before I found that I had no money with me. That was part of it too, you see; I couldn't cash a check. I couldn't get off the truck and go back to town and get some money. I couldn't do that. So I have been walking and bumming rides ever of her bones and the texture of the flesh. "You have your whole life before you, practically. How old are you? You're not past thirty yet." His voice was not loud, almost a whisper.

When she spoke she did not lower her voice at all. She had not moved, her arms still folded across her breast. "Why did you leave your wife?" she said.

"Because she ate shrimp," he said. "I couldn't— You see, it was Friday, and I thought how at noon I'd go to the station and get the box of shrimp off the train and walk home with it, counting a hundred steps and chang- ing hands with it, and it—"

"Did you do that every day?" the woman said.

"No. Just Friday. But I have done it for ten years, since we were married. And I still dont like to smell shrimp. But I wouldn't mind the carrying it home so much. I could stand that. It's because the package drips. All the way home it drips and drips, until after a while I follow myself to the station and stand aside and watch Horace Benbow take that box off the train and start home with it, changing hands every hundred steps, and I following him, thinking Here lies Horace Benbow in a fading series of small stinking spots on a Mississippi sidewalk."

"Oh," the woman said. She breathed quietly, her arms folded. She moved; he gave back and followed her down the hall. They entered the kitchen where a lamp burned. "You'll have to excuse the way I look," the woman said. She went to the box behind the stove and drew it out and stood above it, her hands hidden in the front of her garment. Benbow stood in the middle of the room. "I and rotted leaves and branches. Following Tommy, Benbow walked in a faint path where feet had worn the rotting vegetation down to the clay. Overhead an arching hedgerow of trees thinned against the sky.

The descent increased, curving. "It was about here that we saw the owl," Benbow said.

Ahead of him Tommy guffawed. "It skeered him too, I'll be bound," he said.

"Yes," Benbow said. He followed Tommy's vague shape, trying to walk carefully, to talk carefully, with that tedious concern of drunkenness.

"I be dawg if he aint the skeeriest durn *white* man I ever see," Tommy said. "Here he was comin up the path to the porch and that ere dog come out from under the house and went up and sniffed his heels, like ere a dog will, and I be dawg if he didn't flinch off like it was a moccasin and him barefoot, and whupped out that little artermatic pistol and shot it dead as a door-nail. I be durn if he didn't."

"Whose dog was it?" Horace said.

"Hit was mine," Tommy said. He chortled. "A old dog that wouldn't hurt a flea if hit could."

The road descended and flattened; Benbow's feet whispered into sand, walking carefully. Against the pale sand he could now see Tommy, moving at a shuffling shamble like a mule walks in sand, without seeming effort, his bare feet hissing, flicking the sand back in faint spouting gusts from each inward flick of his toes.

The bulky shadow of the felled tree blobbed across the road. Tommy climbed over it and Benbow followed, still carefully, gingerly, hauling himself through a mass

"Oh," Benbow said. "Well, I think I'd rather starve than have that man around me."

Tommy guffawed. "Popeye's all right. He's just a little curious." He walked on, shapeless against the hushed glare of the road, the sandy road. "I be dawg if he aint a case, now. Aint he?"

"Yes," Benbow said. "He's all of that."

The truck was waiting where the road, clay again, began to mount toward the gravel highway. Two men sat on the fender, smoking cigarettes; overhead the trees thinned against the stars of more than midnight.

"You took your time," one of the men said. "Didn't you? I aimed to be halfway to town by now. I got a woman waiting for me."

"Sure," the other man said. "Waiting on her back." The first man cursed him.

"We come as fast as we could," Tommy said. "Whyn't you fellows hang out a lantern? If me and him had a been the Law, we'd had you, sho."

"Ah, go climb a tree, you mat-faced bastard," the first man said. They snapped their cigarettes away and got into the truck. Tommy guffawed, in undertone. Benbow turned and extended his hand.

"Goodbye," he said. "And much obliged, Mister——"

"My name's Tawmmy," the other said. His limp, calloused hand fumbled into Benbow's and pumped it solemnly once and fumbled away. He stood there, a squat, shapeless figure against the faint glare of the road, while Benbow lifted his foot for the step. He stumbled, catching himself.

··· iii

ON THE next afternoon Benbow was at his sister's home. It was in the country, four miles from Jefferson; the home of her husband's people. She was a widow, with a boy ten years old, living in a big house with her son and the great aunt of her husband: a woman of ninety, who lived in a wheel chair, who was known as Miss Jenny. She and Benbow were at the window, watching his sister and a young man walking in the garden. His sister had been a widow for ten years.

"Why hasn't she ever married again?" Benbow said.

"I ask you," Miss Jenny said. "A young woman needs a man."

"But not that one," Benbow said. He looked at the two people. The man wore flannels and a blue coat; a broad, plumpish young man with a swaggering air, vaguely collegiate. "She seems to like children. Maybe because she has one of her own now. Which one is that? Is that the same one she had last fall?"

stupid, serene face. She was in her customary white dress. "Horace, this is Gowan Stevens," she said. "My brother, Gowan."

"How do you do, sir," Stevens said. He gave Benbow's hand a quick, hard, high, close grip. At that moment the boy, Benbow Sartoris, Benbow's nephew, came in. "I've heard of you," Stevens said.

"Gowan went to Virginia," the boy said.

"Ah," Benbow said. "I've heard of it."

"Thanks," Stevens said. "But everybody cant go to Harvard."

"Thank you," Benbow said. "It was Oxford."

"Horace is always telling folks he went to Oxford so they'll think he means the state university, and he can tell them different," Miss Jenny said.

"Gowan goes to Oxford a lot," the boy said. "He's got a jelly there. He takes her to the dances. Dont you, Gowan?"

"Right, bud," Stevens said. "A red-headed one."

"Hush, Bory," Narcissa said. She looked at her brother. "How are Belle and Little Belle?" She almost said something else, then she ceased. Yet she looked at her brother, her gaze grave and intent.

"If you keep on expecting him to run off from Belle, he will do it," Miss Jenny said. "He'll do it someday. But Narcissa wouldn't be satisfied, even then," she said. "Some women wont want a man to marry a certain woman. But all the women will be mad if he ups and leaves her."

"You hush, now," Narcissa said.

"He should find ample field for gentlemanly drinking there," Horace said. "Gentlemanly anything else. I suppose that's why he is going down ahead of time."

"Taking an old girl to a dance," the boy said. "He's going to Starkville Saturday, to the baseball game. He said he'd take me, but you wont let me go."

the three formal yearly balls, the town boys, lounging in attitudes of belligerent casualness, with their identical hats and upturned collars, watched her enter the gymnasium upon black collegiate arms and vanish in a swirling glitter upon a glittering swirl of music, with her high delicate head and her bold painted mouth and soft chin, her eyes blankly right and left looking, cool, predatory and discreet.

Later, the music wailing beyond the glass, they would watch her through the windows as she passed in swift rotation from one pair of black sleeves to the next, her waist shaped slender and urgent in the interval, her feet filling the rhythmic gap with music. Stooping they would drink from flasks and light cigarettes, then erect again, motionless against the light, the upturned collars, the hatted heads, would be like a row of hatted and muffled busts cut from black tin and nailed to the window-sills.

There would always be three or four of them there when the band played Home, Sweet Home, lounging near the exit, their faces cold, bellicose, a little drawn with sleeplessness, watching the couples emerge in a wan aftermath of motion and noise. Three of them watched Temple and Gowan Stevens come out, into the chill presage of spring dawn. Her face was quite pale, dusted over with recent powder, her hair in spent red curls. Her eyes, all pupil now, rested upon them for a blank moment. Then she lifted her hand in a wan gesture, whether at them or not, none could have said. They did not respond, no flicker in their cold eyes. They watched Gowan slip his arm into hers, and the fleet revelation of flank taillamp, come to a stop at the Coop. The lights went off. After a while the car door slammed. The lights came on; the car moved away. It approached again. They leaned against the rail in a row, their hats slanted against the glare. The broken glass glinted in random sparks. The car drew up and stopped opposite them.

"You gentlemen going to town?" Gowan said, opening the door. They leaned against the rail, then the first said "Much obliged" gruffly and they got in, the two others in the rumble seat, the first beside Gowan.

"Pull over this way," he said. "Somebody broke a bottle there."

"Thanks," Gowan said. The car moved on. "You gentlemen going to Starkville tomorrow to the game?"

The ones in the rumble seat said nothing.

"I dont know," the first said. "I dont reckon so."

"I'm a stranger here," Gowan said. "I ran out of liquor tonight, and I've got a date early in the morning. Can you gentlemen tell me where I could get a quart?"

"It's mighty late," the first said. He turned to the others. "You know anybody he can find this time of night, Doc?"

"Luke might," the third said.

"Where does he live?" Gowan said.

"Go on," the first said. "I'll show you." They crossed the square and drove out of town about a half mile.

"This is the road to Taylor, isn't it?" Gowan said.

"Yes," the first said.

"I've got to drive down there early in the morning," Gowan said. "Got to get there before the special does. You gentlemen not going to the game, you say."

"I reckon not," the first said. "Stop here." A steep slope

" 'Course he didn't," the third said. "Doc's all right. Come on, Doc. Take a drink."

"I dont give a damn," Doc said. "Hand it here."

They returned to town. "The shack'll be open," the first said. "At the depot."

It was a confectionery-lunchroom. It was empty save for a man in a soiled apron. They went to the rear and entered an alcove with a table and four chairs. The man brought four glasses and Coca-Colas. "Can I have some sugar and water and a lemon, Cap?" Gowan said. The man brought them. The others watched Gowan make a whiskey sour. "They taught me to drink it this way," he said. They watched him drink. "Hasn't got much kick, to me," he said, filling his glass from the jar. He drank that.

"You sure do drink it," the third said.

"I learned in a good school." There was a high window. Beyond it the sky was paler, fresher. "Have another, gentlemen," he said, filling his glass again. The others helped themselves moderately. "Up at school they consider it better to go down than to hedge," he said. They watched him drink that one. They saw his nostrils bead suddenly with sweat.

"That's all for him, too," Doc said.

"Who says so?" Gowan said. He poured an inch into the glass. "If we just had some decent liquor. I know a man in my county named Goodwin that makes—"

"That's what they call a drink up at school," Doc said.

Gowan looked at him. "Do you think so? Watch this." He poured into the glass. They watched the liquor rise.

"Look out, fellow," the third said. Gowan filled the glass level full and lifted it and emptied it steadily. He sunlight drove, quite empty of any sense. Then his abdominal muscles completed the retch upon which he had lost consciousness and he heaved himself up and sprawled into the foot of the car, banging his head on the door. The blow fetched him completely to and he opened the door and half fell to the ground and dragged himself up and turned toward the station at a stumbling run. He fell. On hands and knees he looked at the empty siding and up at the sunfilled sky with unbelief and despair. He rose and ran on, in his stained dinner jacket, his burst collar and broken hair. I passed out, he thought in a kind of rage, I passed out. *I passed out.*

The platform was deserted save for a Negro with a broom. "Gret Gawd, white folks," he said.

"The train," Gowan said, "the special. The one that was on that track."

"Hit done lef. But five minutes ago." With the broom still in the arrested gesture of sweeping he watched Gowan turn and run back to the car and tumble into it.

The jar lay on the floor. He kicked it aside and started the engine. He knew that he needed something on his stomach, but there wasn't time. He looked down at the jar. His inside coiled coldly, but he raised the jar and drank, guzzling, choking the stuff down, clapping a cigarette into his mouth to restrain the paroxysm. Almost at once he felt better.

He crossed the square at forty miles an hour. It was six-fifteen. He took the Taylor road, increasing speed. He drank again from the jar without slowing down. When he reached Taylor the train was just pulling out of the station. He slammed in between two wagons as the last neath his dinner jacket. His eyes were bloodshot, puffed, his jowls covered by blue stubble, and looking at him, braced and clinging as the car leaped and bounced in the worn ruts, Temple thought His whiskers have grown since we left Dumfries. It was hair-oil he drank. He bought a bottle of hair-oil at Dumfries and drank it.

He looked at her, feeling her eyes. "Dont get your back up, now. It wont take a minute to run up to Good-win's and get a bottle. It wont take ten minutes. I said I'd get you to Starkville before the train does, and I will. Dont you believe me?"

She said nothing, thinking of the pennant-draped train already in Starkville; of the colorful stands; the band, the yawning glitter of the bass horn; the green diamond dotted with players, crouching, uttering short, yelping cries like marsh-fowl disturbed by an alligator, not certain of where the danger is, motionless, poised, encouraging one another with short meaningless cries, plaintive, wary and forlorn.

"Trying to come over me with your innocent ways. Dont think I spent last night with a couple of your bar-ber-shop jellies for nothing. Dont think I fed them my liquor just because I'm big-hearted. You're pretty good, aren't you? Think you can play around all week with any badger-trimmed hick that owns a Ford, and fool me on Saturday, dont you? Dont think I didn't see your name where it's written on that lavatory wall. Dont you believe me?"

She said nothing, bracing herself as the car lurched from one bank to the other of the cut, going too fast. He was still watching her, making no effort to steer it.

$\mathcal{V}$

THE MAN in overalls was barefoot also. He walked ahead of Temple and Gowan, the shotgun swinging in his hand, his splay feet apparently effortless in the sand into which Temple sank almost to the ankle at each step. From time to time he looked over his shoulder at them, at Gowan's bloody face and splotched clothes, at Temple struggling and lurching on her high heels.

"Putty hard walkin, aint it?" he said. "Ef she'll take off them high heel shoes, she'll git along better."

"Will I?" Temple said. She stopped and stood on alternate legs, holding to Gowan, and removed her slippers. The man watched her, looking at the slippers.

"Durn ef I could git ere two of my fingers into one of them things," he said. "Kin I look at em?" She gave him one. He turned it slowly in his hand. "Durn my hide," he said. He looked at Temple again with his pale, empty gaze. His hair grew innocent and straw-like, bleached on the crown, darkening about his ears and neck in untidy

The man mounted to the porch and set the shotgun just inside the door.

"She's around somewher," he said. He looked at Temple again. "Hit aint no cause fer yo wife to fret," he said. "Lee'll git you to town, I reckon."

Temple looked at him. They looked at one another soberly, like two children or two dogs. "What's your name?"

"My name's Tawmmy," he said. "Hit aint no need to fret."

The hall was open through the house. She entered. "Where you going?" Gowan said. "Why dont you wait out here?" She didn't answer. She went on down the hall. Behind her she could hear Gowan's and the man's voices. The back porch lay in sunlight, a segment of sunlight framed by the door. Beyond, she could see a weed-choked slope and a huge barn, broken-backed, tranquil in sunny desolation. To the right of the door she could see the corner either of a detached building or of a wing of the house. But she could hear no sound save the voices from the front.

She went on, slowly. Then she stopped. On the square of sunlight framed by the door lay the shadow of a man's head, and she half spun, poised with running. But the shadow wore no hat, so she turned and on tiptoe she went to the door and peered around it. A man sat in a splint-bottom chair, in the sunlight, the back of his bald, white-fringed head toward her, his hands crossed on the head of a rough stick. She emerged onto the back porch.

POPEYE WENT ON around the house. Gowan was leaning over the edge of the porch, dabbing gingerly at his bloody nose. The barefooted man squatted on his heels against the wall.

"For Christ's sake," Popeye said, "why cant you take him out back and wash him off? Do you want him sitting around here all day looking like a damn hog with its throat cut?" He snapped the cigarette into the weeds and sat on the top step and began to scrape his muddy shoes with a platinum penknife on the end of his watch chain.

The barefoot man rose.

"You said something about—" Gowan said.

"Pssst!" the other said. He began to wink and frown at Gowan, jerking his head at Popeye's back.

"And then you get on back down that road," Popeye said. "You hear?"

"I thought you was fixin to watch down ther," the man said.

be dawg ef you didn't drive that ere car straight into that tree."

"Come on. Haven't you got some hid out somewhere?"

"Mought be a little in the barn. But dont let him hyear us, er he'll find hit and po hit out." He went back to the door and peered up the hall. Then they left the porch and went toward the barn, crossing what had once been a kitchen garden choked now with cedar and blackjack saplings. Twice the man looked back over his shoulder. The second time he said:

"Yon's yo wife wantin something."

Temple stood in the kitchen door. "Gowan," she called.

"Wave yo hand er somethin," the man said. "Ef she dont hush, he's goin to hyear us." Gowan flapped his hand. They went on and entered the barn. Beside the entrance a crude ladder mounted. "Better wait twell I git up," the man said. "Hit's putty rotten; mought not hold us both."

"Why dont you fix it, then? Dont you use it every day?"

"Hit's helt all right, so fur," the other said. He mounted. Then Gowan followed, through the trap, into yellow-barred gloom where the level sun fell through the broken walls and roof. "Walk wher I do," the man said. "You'll tromp on a loose boa'd and find yoself downstairs befo you know hit." He picked his way across the floor and dug an earthenware jug from a pile of rotting hay in the corner. "One place he wont look fer hit," he said. "Skeered of sp'ilin them gal's hands of hisn."

They drank. "I've seen you out hyer befo," the man said. "Caint call yo name, though."

"Did I tell you to get on down that road, or didn't I?"

"Yeuh," Tommy said. "You told me." Popeye turned without so much as a glance at Gowan. Tommy followed. His back still shook with secret glee. Temple met Popeye halfway to the house. Without ceasing to run she appeared to pause. Even her flapping coat did not overtake her, yet for an appreciable instant she faced Popeye with a grimace of taut, toothed coquetry. He did not stop; the finicking swagger of his narrow back did not falter. Temple ran again. She passed Tommy and clutched Gowan's arm.

"Gowan, I'm scared. She said for me not to— You've been drinking again; you haven't even washed the blood— She says for us to go away from here . . ." Her eyes were quite black, her face small and wan in the dusk. She looked toward the house. Popeye was just turning the corner. "She has to walk all the way to a spring for water; she— They've got the cutest little baby in a box behind the stove. Gowan, she said for me not to be here after dark. She said to ask him. He's got a car. She said she didn't think he—"

"Ask who?" Gowan said. Tommy was looking back at them. Then he went on.

"That black man. She said she didn't think he would, but he might. Come on." They went toward the house. A path led around it to the front. The car was parked between the path and the house, in the tall weeds. Temple faced Gowan again, her hand lying upon the door of the car. "It wont take him any time, in this. I know a boy at home has one. It will run eighty. All he would have to do is just drive us to a town, because she said if we were

Gowan. Then he quit looking at him and Temple said suddenly:

"What river did you fall in with that suit on? Do you have to shave it off at night?" Then she was moving toward the door with Gowan's hand in the small of her back, her head reverted, her heels clattering. Popeye leaned motionless against the post, his head turned over his shoulder in profile.

"Do you want—" Gowan hissed.

"You mean old thing!" Temple cried. "You mean old thing!"

Gowan shoved her into the house. "Do you want him to slam your damn head off?" he said.

"You're scared of him!" Temple said. "You're scared!"

"Shut your mouth!" Gowan said. He began to shake her. Their feet scraped on the bare floor as though they were performing a clumsy dance, and clinging together they lurched into the wall. "Look out," he said, "you're getting all that stuff stirred up in me again." She broke free, running. He leaned against the wall and watched her in silhouette run out the back door.

She ran into the kitchen. It was dark save for a crack of light about the fire door of the stove. She whirled and ran out the door and saw Gowan going down the hill toward the barn. He's going to drink some more, she thought; he's getting drunk again. That makes three times today. Still more dusk had grown in the hall. She stood on tiptoe, listening, thinking I'm hungry, I haven't eaten all day; thinking of the school, the lighted windows, the slow couples strolling toward the sound of the supper bell, and of her father sitting on the porch at home,

vii

FROM SOMEWHERE HERE beyond the lamplit hall she could
hear the voices—a word; now and then a laugh: the
harsh, derisive laugh of a man easily brought to mirth by
youth or by age, cutting across the spluttering of frying
meat on the stove where the woman stood. Once she
heard two of them come down the hall in their heavy
shoes, and a moment later the clatter of the dipper in the
galvanised pail and the voice that had laughed, cursing.
Holding her coat close she peered around the door with
the wide, abashed curiosity of a child, and saw Gowan
and a second man in khaki breeches. He's getting drunk
again, she thought. He's got drunk four times since we left
Taylor.

"Is he your brother?" she said.

"Who?" the woman said. "My what?" She turned the
meat on the hissing skillet.

"I thought maybe your young brother was here."

told him what would happen and I tried to get him to throw the jar away and when we stopped at that little country store to buy a shirt he got drunk again. And so we hadn't eaten and we stopped at Dumfries and he went into the restaurant but I was too worried to eat and I couldn't find him and then he came up another street and I felt the bottle in his pocket before he knocked my hand away. He kept on saying I had his lighter and then when he lost it and I told him he had, he swore he never owned one in his life."

The meat hissed and spluttered in the skillet. "He got drunk three separate times," Temple said. "Three separate times in one day. Buddy—that's Hubert, my youngest brother—said that if he ever caught me with a drunk man, he'd beat hell out of me. And now I'm with one that gets drunk three times in one day." Leaning her hip against the table, her hand crushing the cigarette, she began to laugh. "Dont you think that's funny?" she said. Then she quit laughing by holding her breath, and she could hear the faint guttering the lamp made, and the meat in the skillet and the hissing of the kettle on the stove, and the voices, the harsh, abrupt, meaningless masculine sounds from the house. "And you have to cook for all of them every night. All those men eating here, the house full of them at night, in the dark . . ." She dropped the crushed cigarette. "May I hold the baby? I know how; I'll hold him good." She ran to the box, stooping, and lifted the sleeping child. It opened its eyes, whimpering. "Now, now; Temple's got it." She rocked it, held high and awkward in her thin arms. "Listen," she said, looking at the woman's back, "will you ask him?

can have cars, and when you had a date with a town boy on Friday or Saturday or Sunday, the boys in school wouldn't have a date with you, because they cant have cars. So I had to slip out. And a girl that didn't like me told the Dean, because I had a date with a boy she liked and he never asked her for another date. So I had to."

"If you didn't slip out, you wouldn't get to go riding," the woman said. "Is that it? And now when you slipped out once too often, you're squealing."

"Gowan's not a town boy. He's from Jefferson. He went to Virginia. He kept on saying how they had taught him to drink like a gentleman, and I begged him just to let me out anywhere and lend me enough money for a ticket because I only had two dollars, but he—"

"Oh, I know your sort," the woman said. "Honest women. Too good to have anything to do with common people. You'll slip out at night with the kids, but just let a man come along." She turned the meat. "Take all you can get, and give nothing. 'I'm a pure girl; I dont do that.' You'll slip out with the kids and burn their gasoline and eat their food, but just let a man so much as look at you and you faint away because your father the judge and your four brothers might not like it. But just let you get into a jam, then who do you come crying to? to us, the ones that are not good enough to lace the judge's almighty shoes." Across the child Temple gazed at the woman's back, her face like a small pale mask beneath the precarious hat.

"My brother said he would kill Frank. He didn't say he would give me a whipping if he caught me with him; he said he would kill the goddam son of a bitch in his yellow and they sent him to Leavenworth. Then the war came and they let him out to go to it. He got two medals, and when it was over they put him back in Leavenworth until the lawyer got a congressman to get him out. Then I could quit jazzing again—"

"Jazzing?" Temple whispered, holding the child, looking herself no more than an elongated and leggy infant in her scant dress and uptilted hat.

"Yes, putty-face!" the woman said. "How do you suppose I paid that lawyer? And that's the sort of man you think will care that much—" with the fork in her hand she came and snapped her fingers softly and viciously in Temple's face "—what happens to you. And you, you little doll-faced slut, that think you cant come into a room where a man is without him . . ." Beneath the faded garment her breast moved deep and full. With her hands on her hips she looked at Temple with cold, blazing eyes. "Man? You've never seen a real man. You dont know what it is to be wanted by a real man. And thank your stars you haven't and never will, for then you'd find just what that little putty face is worth, and all the rest of it you think you are jealous of when you're just scared of it. And if he is just man enough to call you whore, you'll say Yes Yes and you'll crawl naked in the dirt and the mire for him to call you that. . . . Give me that baby." Temple held the child, gazing at the woman, her mouth moving as if she were saying Yes Yes Yes. The woman threw the fork onto the table. "Turn loose," she said, lifting the child. It opened its eyes and wailed. The woman drew a chair out and sat down, the child upon her lap. "Will you hand me one of those diapers on the line yon-dog after every hot little bitch that comes along? It's you."

"Yes. I'll go anywhere."

"I know your sort. I've seen them. All running, but not too fast. Not so fast you cant tell a real man when you see him. Do you think you've got the only one in the world?"

"Gowan," Temple whispered, "Gowan."

"I have slaved for that man," the woman whispered, her lips scarce moving, in her still, dispassionate voice. It was as though she were reciting a formula for bread. "I worked night shift as a waitress so I could see him Sundays at the prison. I lived two years in a single room, cooking over a gas-jet, because I promised him. I lied to him and made money to get him out of prison, and when I told him how I made it, he beat me. And now you must come here where you're not wanted. Nobody asked you to come here. Nobody cares whether you are afraid or not. Afraid? You haven't the guts to be really afraid, any more than you have to be in love."

"I'll pay you," Temple whispered. "Anything you say. My father will give it to me." The woman watched her, her face motionless, as rigid as when she had been speaking. "I'll send you clothes. I have a new fur coat. I just wore it since Christmas. It's as good as new."

The woman laughed. Her mouth laughed, with no sound, no movement of her face. "Clothes? I had three fur coats once. I gave one of them to a woman in an alley by a saloon. Clothes? God." She turned suddenly. "I'll get a car. You get away from here and dont you ever come back. Do you hear?"

trampling of feet in the hall, a rasping of chairs, the voice of the man who had laughed above them, laughing again. She turned, motionless again, watching the door. The woman entered.

"Go and eat your supper," she said.

"The car," Temple said. "I could go now, while they're eating."

"What car?" the woman said. "Go on and eat. Nobody's going to hurt you."

"I'm not hungry. I haven't eaten today. I'm not hungry at all."

"Go and eat your supper," she said.

"I'll wait and eat when you do."

"Go on and eat your supper. I've got to get done here some time tonight."

Gowan stood up, propping himself on the table. She began to resist, grinning at Tommy, picking at the man's fingers.

"Quit that, Van," Goodwin said.

"Right on my lap here," Van said.

"Let her go," Goodwin said.

"Who'll make me?" Van said. "Who's big enough?"

"Let her go," Goodwin said. Then she was free. She began to back slowly away. Behind her the woman, entering with a dish, stepped aside. Still smiling her aching, rigid grimace Temple backed from the room. In the hall she whirled and ran. She ran right off the porch, into the weeds, and sped on. She ran to the road and down it for fifty yards in the darkness, then without a break she whirled and ran back to the house and sprang onto the porch and crouched against the door just as someone came up the hall. It was Tommy.

"Oh, hyer you are," he said. He thrust something awkwardly at her. "Hyer," he said.

"What is it?" she whispered.

"Little bite of victuals. I bet you aint et since mawnin."

"No. Not then, even," she whispered.

"You eat a little mite and you'll feel better," he said, poking the plate at her. "You set down hyer and eat a little bite wher wont nobody bother you. Durn them fellers."

Temple leaned around the door, past his dim shape, her face wan as a small ghost in the refracted light from the dining-room. "Mrs—Mrs . . ." she whispered.

"She's in the kitchen. Want me to go back there with you?" In the dining-room a chair scraped. Between blinks me to call Lee?" Van stood against the light, in a khaki shirt and breeches, a cigarette behind his ear against the smooth sweep of his blond hair. Beyond him Temple stood behind the chair in which the woman sat at the table, her mouth open a little, her eyes quite black.

When Tommy went back to the porch with the jug he said to Goodwin: "Why dont them fellers quit pesterin that gal?"

"Who's pestering her?"

"Van is. She's skeered. Whyn't they leave her be?"

"It's none of your business. You keep out of it. You hear?"

"Them fellers ought to quit pesterin her," Tommy said. He squatted against the wall. They were drinking, passing the jug back and forth, talking. With the top of his mind he listened to them, to Van's gross and stupid tales of city life with rapt interest, guffawing now and then, drinking in his turn. Van and Gowan were doing the talking, and Tommy listened to them. "Them two's fixin to have hit out with one another," he whispered to Goodwin in a chair beside him. "Hyear em?" They were talking quite loud; Goodwin moved swiftly and lightly from his chair, his feet striking the floor with light thuds; Tommy saw Van standing and Gowan holding himself erect by the back of his chair.

"I never meant—" Van said.

"Dont say it, then," Goodwin said.

Gowan said something. That durn feller, Tommy thought. Cant even talk no more.

"Shut up, you," Goodwin said.

Temple was sitting on the bed, her legs tucked under her, erect, her hands lying in her lap, her hat tilted on the back of her head. She looked quite small, her very attitude an outrage to muscle and tissue of more than seventeen and more compatible with eight or ten, her elbows close to her sides, her face turned toward the door against which a chair was wedged. There was nothing in the room save the bed, with its faded patchwork quilt, and the chair. The walls had been plastered once, but the plaster had cracked and fallen in places, exposing the lathing and molded shreds of cloth. On the wall hung a raincoat and a khaki-covered canteen.

Temple's head began to move. It turned slowly, as if she were following the passage of someone beyond the wall. It turned on to an excruciating degree, though no other muscle moved, like one of those papier-mâché Easter toys filled with candy, and became motionless in that reverted position. Then it turned back, slowly, as though pacing invisible feet beyond the wall, back to the chair against the door and became motionless there for a moment. Then she faced forward and Tommy watched her take a tiny watch from the top of her stocking and look at it. With the watch in her hand she lifted her head and looked directly at him, her eyes calm and empty as two holes. After a while she looked down at the watch again and returned it to her stocking.

She rose from the bed and removed her coat and stood motionless, arrowlike in her scant dress, her head bent, her hands clasped before her. She sat on the bed again. She sat with her legs close together, her head bent. She raised her head and looked about the room.

slippers beside her head and drew the raincoat about her legs and lay down, drawing the quilt up, then she sat up and removed the hat and shook her hair out and laid the hat with the other garments and prepared to lie down again. Again she paused. She opened the raincoat and produced a compact from somewhere and, watching her motions in the tiny mirror, she spread and fluffed her hair with her fingers and powdered her face and replaced the compact and looked at the watch again and fastened the raincoat. She moved the garments one by one under the quilt and lay down and drew the quilt to her chin. The voices had got quiet for a moment and in the silence Tommy could hear a faint, steady chatter of the shucks inside the mattress where Temple lay, her hands crossed on her breast and her legs straight and close and deco-rous, like an effigy on an ancient tomb.

The voices were still; he had completely forgot them until he heard Goodwin say "Stop it. Stop that!" A chair crashed over; he heard Goodwin's light thudding feet; the chair clattered along the porch as though it had been kicked aside, and crouching, his elbows out a little in squat, bear-like alertness, Tommy heard dry, light sounds like billiard balls. "Tommy," Goodwin said.

When necessary he could move with that thick, light-ning-like celerity of badgers or coons. He was around the house and on the porch in time to see Gowan slam into the wall and slump along it and plunge full length off the porch into the weeds, and Popeye in the door, his head thrust forward. "Grab him there!" Goodwin said. Tommy sprang upon Popeye in a sidling rush.

broken about his face, long as a girl's. He flung it back with a toss of his head. His chin was bloody and he deliberately spat blood onto the floor.

"Go on," Goodwin said, carrying Gowan's shoulders, "put him on the bed." They swung Gowan onto the bed. His bloody head lolled over the edge. Van jerked him over and slammed him into the mattress. He groaned, lifting his hand. Van struck him across the face with his palm.

"Lie still, you—"

"Let be," Goodwin said. He caught Van's hand. For an instant they glared at one another.

"I said, Let be," Goodwin said. "Get out of here."

"Got proteck . . ." Gowan muttered ". . . girl. 'Ginia gem . . . gemman got proteck . . ."

"Get out of here, now," Goodwin said.

The woman stood in the door beside Tommy, her back against the door frame. Beneath a cheap coat her nightdress dropped to her feet.

Van lifted Temple's dress from the bed. "Van," Goodwin said. "I said get out."

"I heard you," Van said. He shook the dress out. Then he looked at Temple in the corner, her arms crossed, her hands clutching her shoulders. Goodwin moved toward Van. He dropped the dress and went around the bed. Popeye came in the door, a cigarette in his fingers. Beside the woman Tommy drew his breath hissing through his ragged teeth.

He saw Van take hold of the raincoat upon Temple's breast and rip it open. Then Goodwin sprang between them; he saw Van duck, whirling, and Temple fumbling

"While you finish the trick Van started and you wouldn't let him finish? You poor fool. You poor fool."

"Come on, now," he said, his hand on her shoulder. "Go back to bed."

"But dont come back. Dont bother to come back. I wont be there. You owe me nothing. Dont think you do."

Goodwin took her wrists and drew them steadily apart. Slowly and steadily he carried her hands around behind her and held them in one of his. With the other hand he opened the coat. The nightdress was of faded pink crepe, lace-trimmed, laundered and laundered until, like the garment on the wire, the lace was a fibrous mass.

"Hah," he said. "Dressed for company."

"Whose fault is it if this is the only one I have? Whose fault is it? Not mine. I've given them away to nigger maids after one night. But do you think any nigger would take this and not laugh in my face?"

He let the coat fall to. He released her hands and she drew the coat together. With his hand on her shoulder he began to push her toward the door. "Go on," he said. Her shoulder gave. It alone moved, her body turning on her hips, her face reverted, watching him. "Go on," he said. But her torso alone turned, her hips and head still touching the wall. He turned and crossed the room and went swiftly around the bed and caught Temple by the front of the raincoat with one hand. He began to shake her. Holding her up by the gathered wad of coat he shook her, her small body clattering soundlessly inside the loose garment, her shoulders and thighs thumping against the wall. "You little fool!" he said. "You little and a burning cigarette. Tommy squatted outside the door, in the darkness.

He was there when Goodwin came out with the rain-coat. Goodwin entered the kitchen without seeing him. "Where's Tommy?" he said. Tommy heard Popeye say something, then Goodwin emerged with Van following him, the raincoat on his arm now. "Come on, now," Goodwin said. "Let's get that stuff out of here."

Tommy's pale eyes began to glow faintly, like those of a cat. The woman could see them in the darkness when he crept into the room after Popeye, and while Popeye stood over the bed where Temple lay. They glowed sud-denly out of the darkness at her, then they went away and she could hear him breathing beside her; again they glowed up at her with a quality furious and ques-tioning and sad and went away again and he crept be-hind Popeye from the room.

He saw Popeye return to the kitchen, but he did not follow at once. He stopped at the hall door and squatted there. His body began to writhe again in shocked inde-cision, his bare feet whispering on the floor with a faint, rocking movement as he swayed from side to side, his hands wringing slowly against his flanks. And Lee too, he said, And Lee too. Durn them fellers. Durn them fellers. Twice he stole along the porch until he could see the shadow of Popeye's hat on the kitchen floor, then re-turned to the hall and the door beyond which Temple lay and Gowan snored. The third time he smelled Pop-eye's cigarette. Ef he'll jest keep that up, he said. And Lee too, he said, rocking from side to side in a dull, ex-cruciating agony, And Lee too.

ix

THE ROOM was dark. The woman stood inside the door, against the wall, in the cheap coat, the lace-trimmed crepe nightgown, just inside the lockless door. She could hear Gowan snoring in the bed, and the other men moving about, on the porch and in the hall and in the kitchen, talking, their voices indistinguishable through the door. After a while they got quiet. Then she could hear nothing at all save Gowan as he choked and snored and moaned through his battered nose and face.

She heard the door open. The man came in, without trying to be silent. He entered, passing within a foot of her. She knew it was Goodwin before he spoke. He went to the bed. "I want the raincoat," he said. "Sit up and take it off." The woman could hear the shucks in the mattress as Temple sat up and Goodwin took the raincoat off of her. He returned across the floor and went out.

She stood just inside the door. She could tell all of them by the way they breathed. Then, without having

"You fool!" the woman said in a thin, fierce whisper. "It's me. It's just me."

Temple ceased to roll her head, but she still thrashed from side to side beneath the woman's hand. "I'll tell my father!" she said. "I'll tell my father!"

The woman held her. "Get up," she said. Temple ceased to struggle. She lay still, rigid. The woman could hear her wild breathing. "Will you get up and walk quiet?" the woman said.

"Yes!" Temple said. "Will you get me out of here? Will you? Will you?"

"Yes," the woman said. "Get up." Temple got up, the shucks whispering. In the further darkness Gowan snored, savage and profound. At first Temple couldn't stand alone. The woman held her up. "Stop it," the woman said. "You've got to stop it. You've got to be quiet."

"I want my clothes," Temple whispered. "I haven't got anything on but . . ."

"Do you want your clothes," the woman said, "or do you want to get out of here?"

"Yes," Temple said. "Anything. If you'll just get me out of here."

On their bare feet they moved like ghosts. They left the house and crossed the porch and went on toward the barn. When they were about fifty yards from the house the woman stopped and turned and jerked Temple up to her, and gripping her by the shoulders, their faces close together, she cursed Temple in a whisper, a sound no louder than a sigh and filled with fury. Then she flung her away and they went on. They entered the hallway. It

WHILE THE WOMAN was cooking breakfast, the child still
—or already—asleep in the box behind the stove, she
heard a blundering sound approaching across the porch
and stop at the door. When she looked around she saw
the wild and battered and bloody apparition which she
recognised as Gowan. His face, beneath a two days' stubble, was marked, his lip was cut. One eye was closed and
the front of his shirt and coat were blood-stained to the
waist. Through his swollen and stiffened lips he was trying to say something. At first the woman could not
understand a word. "Go and bathe your face," she said.
"Wait. Come in here and sit down. I'll get the basin."

He looked at her, trying to talk. "Oh," the woman said.
"She's all right. She's down there in the crib, asleep."
She had to repeat it three or four times, patiently. "In
the crib. Asleep. I stayed with her until daylight. Go
wash your face, now."

in the cold water and trying to examine his reflection in the broken surface, whispering Jesus Christ to himself in a kind of despair. He thought about returning to the house for a drink, then he thought of having to face Temple, the men; of Temple there among them.

When he reached the highroad the sun was well up, warm. I'll get cleaned up some, he said. And come back with another car to get her. I'll decide what to say to her on the way to town; thinking of Temple returning among people who knew him, who might know him. I passed out twice, he said. *I passed out twice.* Jesus Christ, Jesus Christ he whispered, his body writhing inside his disreputable and bloody clothes in an agony of rage and shame.

His head began to clear with air and motion, but as he began to feel better physically the blackness of the future increased. Town, the world, began to appear as a black cul-de-sac; a place in which he must walk forever more, his whole body cringing and flinching from whispering eyes when he had passed, and when in midmorning he reached the house he sought, the prospect of facing Temple again was more than he could bear. So he engaged the car and directed the man and paid him and went on. A little later a car going in the opposite direction stopped and picked him up.

she could not pull it open, her numb hands scoring at the
undressed planks until she could hear her fingernails. It
swung back and she sprang out. At once she sprang back
into the crib and banged the door to. The blind man was
coming down the slope at a scuffling trot, tapping
ahead with the stick, the other hand at his waist, clutching a wad of his trousers. He passed the crib with his
braces dangling about his hips, his gymnasium shoes
scuffing in the dry chaff of the hallway, and passed from
view, the stick rattling lightly along the rank of empty
stalls.

Temple crouched against the door, clutching her coat
about her. She could hear him back there in one of the
stalls. She opened the door and peered out, at the house
in the bright May sunshine, the sabbath peace, and she
thought about the girls and men leaving the dormitories
in their new spring clothes, strolling along the shaded
streets toward the cool, unhurried sound of bells. She
lifted her foot and examined the soiled sole of her stocking, brushing at it with her palm, then at the other one.

The blind man's stick clattered again. She jerked her
head back and closed the door to a crack and watched
him pass, slower now, hunching his braces onto his shoulders. He mounted the slope and entered the house. Then
she opened the door and stepped gingerly down.

She walked swiftly to the house, her stockinged feet
flinching and cringing from the rough earth, watching
the house. She mounted to the porch and entered the
kitchen and stopped, listening into the silence. The stove
was cold. Upon it the blackened coffee-pot sat, and a
soiled skillet; upon the table soiled dishes were piled at

quite a woman—she moved swiftly, smoothing her stock-
ings and writhing into her scant, narrow dress. Now I
can stand anything, she thought quietly, with a kind of
dull, spent astonishment; I can stand just anything. From
the top of one stocking she removed a watch on a broken
black ribbon. Nine oclock. With her fingers she combed
her matted curls, combing out three or four cottonseed-
hulls. She took up the coat and hat and listened again at
the door.

She returned to the back porch. In the basin was a
residue of dirty water. She rinsed it and filled it and
bathed her face. A soiled towel hung from a nail. She
used it gingerly, then she took a compact from her coat
and was using it when she found the woman watching
her in the kitchen door.

"Good morning," Temple said. The woman held the
child on her hip. It was asleep. "Hello, baby," Temple
said, stooping; "you wan s'eep all day? Look at Temple."
They entered the kitchen. The woman poured coffee into
a cup.

"It's cold, I expect," she said. "Unless you want to make
up the fire." From the oven she took a pan of bread.

"No," Temple said, sipping the lukewarm coffee, feeling her insides move in small, tickling clots, like loose
shot. "I'm not hungry. I haven't eaten in two days, but
I'm not hungry. Isn't that funny? I haven't eaten in . . ."
She looked at the woman's back with a fixed placative
grimace. "You haven't got a bathroom, have you?"

"What?" the woman said. She looked at Temple
across her shoulder while Temple stared at her with that
grimace of cringing and placative assurance. From a

runlet to where a jutting shoulder formed a nook matted with briers. Among the new green last year's dead leaves from the branches overhead clung, not yet fallen to earth. She stood here for a while, folding and folding the sheets in her fingers, in a kind of despair. When she rose she saw, upon the glittering mass of leaves along the crest of the ditch, the squatting outline of a man.

For an instant she stood and watched herself run out of her body, out of one slipper. She watched her legs twinkle against the sand, through the flecks of sunlight, for several yards, then whirl and run back and snatch up the slipper and whirl and run again.

When she caught a glimpse of the house she was opposite the front porch. The blind man sat in a chair, his face lifted into the sun. At the edge of the woods she stopped and put on the slipper. She crossed the ruined lawn and sprang onto the porch and ran down the hall. When she reached the back porch she saw a man in the door of the barn, looking toward the house. She crossed the porch in two strides and entered the kitchen, where the woman sat at the table, smoking, the child on her lap.

"He was watching me!" Temple said. "He was watching me all the time!" She leaned beside the door, peering out, then she came to the woman, her face small and pale, her eyes like holes burned with a cigar, and laid her hand on the cold stove.

"Who was?" the woman said.

"Yes," Temple said. "He was there in the bushes, watching me all the time." She looked toward the door, then back at the woman, and saw her hand lying on the stove.

hulls and a few scattered corn-cobs gnawed bone-clean. Something thudded against the wall and struck her hand in ricochet. The rat was in that corner now, on the floor. Again their faces were not twelve inches apart, the rat's eyes glowing and fading as though worked by lungs. Then it stood erect, its back to the corner, its forepaws curled against its chest, and began to squeak at her in tiny plaintive gasps. She backed away on hands and knees, watching it. Then she got to her feet and sprang at the door, hammering at it, watching the rat over her shoulder, her body arched against the door, rasping at the planks with her bare hands.

the first position of a dance, they stood in a mounting terrific muscular hiatus.

With scarce any movement at all he flung her aside in a complete revolution that fetched her up against the table, her arm flung back for balance, her body bent and her hand fumbling behind her among the soiled dishes, watching him across the inert body of the child. He walked toward her. "Stand back," she said, lifting her hand slightly, bringing the butcher knife into view. "Stand back." He came steadily toward her, then she struck at him with the knife.

He caught her wrist. She began to struggle. He plucked the child from her and laid it on the table and caught her other hand as it flicked at his face, and holding both wrists in one hand, he slapped her. It made a dry, flat sound. He slapped her again, first on one cheek, then the other, rocking her head from side to side. "That's what I do to them," he said, slapping her. "See?" He released her. She stumbled backward against the table and caught up the child and half crouched between the table and the wall, watching him as he turned and left the room.

She knelt in the corner, holding the child. It had not stirred. She laid her palm first on one cheek, then on the other. She rose and laid the child in the box and took a sunbonnet from a nail and put it on. From another nail she took a coat trimmed with what had once been white fur, and took up the child and left the room.

Tommy was standing in the barn, beside the crib, looking toward the house. The old man sat on the front porch, in the sun. She went down the steps and followed toward the barn. Popeye stopped at the edge of the wood and looked at Goodwin's back. He put another cigarette into his mouth and thrust his fingers into his vest. He went on across the orchard, walking gingerly. Goodwin heard him and looked over his shoulder. Popeye took a match from his vest, flicked it into flame and lit the cigarette. Goodwin looked toward the barn again and Popeye stood at his shoulder, looking toward the barn.

"Who's down there?" he said. Goodwin said nothing. Popeye jetted smoke from his nostrils. "I'm clearing out," he said. Goodwin said nothing, watching the barn. "I said, I'm getting out of here," Popeye said. Without turning his head Goodwin cursed him. Popeye smoked quietly, the cigarette wreathing across his still, soft, black gaze. Then he turned and went toward the house. The old man sat in the sun. Popeye did not enter the house. Instead he went on across the lawn and into the cedars until he was hidden from the house. Then he turned and crossed the garden and the weed-choked lot and entered the barn from the rear.

Tommy squatted on his heels beside the crib door, looking toward the house. Popeye looked at him a while, smoking. Then he snapped the cigarette away and entered a stall quietly. Above the manger was a wooden rack for hay, just under an opening in the loft floor. Popeye climbed into the rack and drew himself silently into the loft, his tight coat strained into thin ridges across his narrow shoulders and back.

"You mean fer me not to let none of them in hyer?"

"All right. I'm not scared of rats. You stay there and dont let him in."

"All right. I'll fix hit so caint nobody git to you. I'll be right hyer."

"All right. Shut the door. Dont let him in here."

"All right." He shut the door. She leaned in it, looking toward the house. He pushed her back so he could close the door. "Hit aint goin to hurt you none, Lee says. All you got to do is lay down."

"All right. I will. Dont you let him in here." The door closed. She heard him drive the hasp to. Then he shook the door.

"Hit's fastened," he said. "Caint nobody git to you now. I'll be right hyer."

He squatted on his heels in the chaff, looking at the house. After a while he saw Goodwin come to the back door and look toward him, and squatting, clasping his knees, Tommy's eyes glowed again, the pale irises appearing for an instant to spin on the pupils like tiny wheels. He squatted there, his lip lifted a little, until Goodwin went back into the house. Then he sighed, expelling his breath, and he looked at the blank door of the crib and again his eyes glowed with a diffident, groping, hungry fire and he began to rub his hands slowly on his shanks, rocking a little from side to side. Then he ceased, became rigid, and watched Goodwin move swiftly across the corner of the house and into the cedars. He squatted rigid, his lip lifted a little upon his ragged teeth.

Sitting in the cottonseed-hulls, in the litter of gnawed

scene, the instant, with a profound finality, completely isolating it, and she sat there, her legs straight before her, her hands limp and palm-up on her lap, looking at Popeye's tight back and the ridges of his coat across the shoulders as he leaned out the door, the pistol behind him, against his flank, wisping thinly along his leg.

He turned and looked at her. He waggled the pistol slightly and put it back in his coat, then he walked toward her. Moving, he made no sound at all; the released door yawned and clapped against the jamb, but it made no sound either; it was as though sound and silence had become inverted. She could hear silence in a thick rustling as he moved toward her through it, thrusting it aside, and she began to say Something is going to happen to me. She was saying it to the old man with the yellow clots for eyes. "Something is happening to me!" she screamed at him, sitting in his chair in the sunlight, his hands crossed on the top of the stick. "I told you it was!" she screamed, voiding the words like hot silent bubbles into the bright silence about them until he turned his head and the two phlegm-clots above her where she lay tossing and thrashing on the rough, sunny boards. "I told you! I told you all the time!"

sun. When she entered the hall, she was walking fast. She was not aware of the child's thin weight. She found Goodwin in their bedroom. He was in the act of putting on a frayed tie; looking at him, she saw that he had just shaved.

"Yes," she said. "What is it? What is it?"

"I've got to walk up to Tull's and telephone for the sheriff," he said.

"The sheriff," she said. "Yes. All right." She came to the bed and laid the child carefully down. "To Tull's," she said. "Yes. He's got a phone."

"You'll have to cook," Goodwin said. "There's Pap."

"You can give him some cold bread. He wont mind. There's some left in the stove. He wont mind."

"I'll go," Goodwin said. "You stay here."

"To Tull's," she said. "All right." Tull was the man at whose house Gowan had found a car. It was two miles away. Tull's family was at dinner. They asked her to stop. "I just want to use the telephone," she said. The telephone was in the dining-room, where they were eating. She called, with them sitting about the table. She didn't know the number. "The Sheriff," she said patiently into the mouthpiece. Then she got the sheriff, with Tull's family sitting about the table, about the Sunday dinner. "A dead man. You pass Mr Tull's about a mile and turn off to the right. . . . Yes, the Old Frenchman place. Yes. This is Mrs Goodwin talking . . . Goodwin. Yes."

He did not rise. He sat with something of the air of a guilty small boy. "How did you—" he said. "Did Belle—"

"Of course. She wired me Saturday. That you had left, and if you came here, to tell you that she had gone back home to Kentucky and had sent for Little Belle."

"Ah, damnation," Benbow said.

"Why?" his sister said. "You want to leave home yourself, but you dont want her to leave."

He stayed at his sister's two days. She had never been given to talking, living a life of serene vegetation like perpetual corn or wheat in a sheltered garden instead of a field, and during those two days she came and went about the house with an air of tranquil and faintly ludicrous tragic disapproval.

After supper they sat in Miss Jenny's room, where Narcissa would read the Memphis paper before taking the boy off to bed. When she went out of the room, Miss Jenny looked at Benbow.

"Go back home, Horace," she said.

"Not to Kinston," Benbow said. "I hadn't intended to stay here, anyway. It wasn't Narcissa I was running to. I haven't quit one woman to run to the skirts of another."

"If you keep on telling yourself that you may believe it, someday," Miss Jenny said. "Then what'll you do?"

"You're right," Benbow said. "Then I'd have to stay at home."

His sister returned. She entered the room with a definite air. "Now for it," Benbow said. His sister had not spoken directly to him all day.

"What are you going to do, Horace?" she said. "You

"You could feel the pistol on him just like you knew he had a navel," Benbow said. "He wouldn't drink, because he said it made him sick to his stomach like a dog; he wouldn't stay and talk with us; he wouldn't do anything: just lurking about, smoking his cigarettes, like a sullen and sick child.

"Goodwin and I were both talking. He had been a cavalry sergeant in the Philippines and on the Border, and in an infantry regiment in France; he never told me why he changed, transferred to infantry and lost his rank. He might have killed someone, might have deserted. He was talking about Manila and Mexican girls, and that halfwit chortling and glugging at the jug and shoving it at me: 'Take some mo'; and then I knew that the woman was just behind the door, listening to us. They are not married. I know that just like I know that that little black man had that flat little pistol in his coat pocket. But she's out there, doing a nigger's work, that's owned diamonds and automobiles too in her day, and bought them with a harder currency than cash. And that blind man, that old man sitting there at the table, waiting for some-body to feed him, with that immobility of blind people, like it was the backs of their eyeballs you looked at while they were hearing music you couldn't hear; that Good-win led out of the room and completely off the earth, as far as I know. I never saw him again. I never knew who he was, who he was kin to. Maybe not to anybody. Maybe that old Frenchman that built the house a hun-dred years ago didn't want him either and just left him there when he died or moved away."

day. He removed the overalls and dressed and left the house.

The street opened into a broader one. To the left it went on to the square, the opening between two build-ings black with a slow, continuous throng, like two streams of ants, above which the cupola of the court-house rose from a clump of oaks and locusts covered with ragged snow. He went on toward the square. Empty wagons still passed him and he passed still more women on foot, black and white, unmistakable by the unease of their garments as well as by their method of walking, be-lieving that town dwellers would take them for town dwellers too, not even fooling one another.

The adjacent alleys were choked with tethered wagons, the teams reversed and nuzzling gnawed corn-ears over the tail-boards. The square was lined two-deep with ranked cars, while the owners of them and of the wagons thronged in slow overalls and khaki, in mail-order scarves and parasols, in and out of the stores, soil-ing the pavement with fruit- and peanut-hulls. Slow as sheep they moved, tranquil, impassable, filling the pas-sages, contemplating the fretful hurrying of those in ur-ban shirts and collars with the large, mild inscrutability of cattle or of gods, functioning outside of time, having left time lying upon the slow and imponderable land green with corn and cotton in the yellow afternoon.

Horace moved among them, swept here and there by the deliberate current, without impatience. Some of them he knew; most of the merchants and professional men remembered him as a boy, a youth, a brother lawyer—

years about the countryside, nor the merchants who on infrequent Saturdays had seen him in town, barefoot, hatless, with his rapt, empty gaze and his cheek bulged innocently by a peppermint jawbreaker. For all general knowledge, he had none.

mo! Den dey ghy stroy de bes ba'ytone singer in nawth Mississippi!"

Sometimes during the day he would lean there, singing alone then, though after a while one or two ragamuffin boys or Negroes with delivery baskets like as not, would halt at the fence, and the white men sitting in tilted chairs along the oil-foul wall of the garage across the street would listen above their steady jaws. "One day mo! Den Ise a gawn po sonnen bitch. Say, Aint no place fer you in heavum! Say, Aint no place fer you in hell! Say, Aint no place fer you in jail!"

"Damn that fellow," Goodwin said, jerking up his black head, his gaunt, brown, faintly harried face. "I aint in any position to wish any man that sort of luck, but I'll be damned. . . ." He wouldn't talk. "I didn't do it. You know that, yourself. You know I wouldn't have. I aint going to say what I think. I didn't do it. They've got to hang it on me first. Let them do that. I'm clear. But if I talk, if I say what I think or believe, I wont be clear." He was sitting on the cot in his cell. He looked up at the windows: two orifices not much larger than sabre slashes.

"Is he that good a shot?" Benbow said. "To hit a man through one of those windows?"

Goodwin looked at him. "Who?"

"Popeye," Benbow said.

"Did Popeye do it?" Goodwin said.

"Didn't he?" Benbow said.

"I've told all I'm going to tell. I dont have to clear my-self; it's up to them to hang it on me."

"Then what do you want with a lawyer?" Benbow said. "What do you want me to do?"

her voice, furious. "When you took another man's wife and child away from him I thought it was dreadful, but I said At least he will not have the face to ever come back here again. And when you just walked out of the house like a nigger and left her I thought that was dreadful too, but I would not let myself believe you meant to leave her for good. And then when you insisted without any reason at all on leaving here and opening the house, scrubbing it yourself and all the town looking on and living there like a tramp, refusing to stay here where everybody would expect you to stay and think it funny when you wouldn't; and now to deliberately mix yourself up with a woman you said yourself was a street-walker, a murderer's woman."

"I cant help it. She has nothing, no one. In a made-over dress all neatly about five years out of mode, and that child that never has been more than half alive, wrapped in a piece of blanket scrubbed almost cotton-white. Asking nothing of anyone except to be let alone, trying to make something out of her life when all you sheltered chaste women—"

"Do you mean to say a moonshiner hasn't got the money to hire the best lawyer in the country?" Miss Jenny said.

"It's not that," Horace said. "I'm sure he could get a better lawyer. It's that—"

"Horace," his sister said. She had been watching him. "Where is that woman?" Miss Jenny was watching him too, sitting a little forward in the wheel chair. "Did you take that woman into my house?"

"It's my house too, honey." She did not know that for

town now and take her to the hotel and get her settled. It's not late."

"And go on back to Kinston until the whole thing is over," Narcissa said. "These people are not your people. Why must you do such things?"

"I cannot stand idly by and see injustice—"

"You wont ever catch up with injustice, Horace," Miss Jenny said.

"Well, that irony which lurks in events, then."

"Hmmph," Miss Jenny said. "It must be because she is one woman you know that dont know anything about that shrimp."

"Anyway, I've talked too much, as usual," Horace said. "So I'll have to trust you all—"

"Fiddlesticks," Miss Jenny said. "Do you think Narcissa'd want anybody to know that any of her folks could know people that would do anything as natural as make love or rob or steal?" There was that quality about his sister. During all the four days between Kinston and Jefferson he had counted on that imperviousness. He hadn't expected her—any woman—to bother very much over a man she had neither married nor borne when she had one she did bear to cherish and fret over. But he had expected that imperviousness, since she had had it thirty-six years.

When he reached the house in town a light burned in one room. He entered, crossing floors which he had scrubbed himself, revealing at the time no more skill with a mop than he had expected, than he had with the lost hammer with which he nailed the windows down and the shutters to ten years ago, who could not even learn and the woman—in the kitchen lighted by a cracked and smutty lamp on a table of clean, spartan dishes and Goodwin and Popeye somewhere in the outer darkness peaceful with insects and frogs yet filled too with Popeye's presence in black and nameless threat. The woman drew the box out from behind the stove and stood above it, her hands still hidden in her shapeless garment. "I have to keep him in this so the rats cant get to him," she said.

"Oh," Horace said, "you have a son." Then she showed him her hands, flung them out in a gesture at once spontaneous and diffident and self-conscious and proud, and told him he might bring her an orange-stick.

She returned, with something wrapped discreetly in a piece of newspaper. He knew that it was a diaper, freshly washed, even before she said: "I made a fire in the stove. I guess I overstepped."

"Of course not," he said. "It's merely a matter of legal precaution, you see," he said. "Better to put everybody to a little temporary discomfort than to jeopardize our case." She did not appear to be listening. She spread the blanket on the bed and lifted the child onto it. "You understand how it is," Horace said. "If the judge suspected that I knew more about it than the facts would warrant—I mean, we must try to give everybody the idea that holding Lee for that killing is just—"

"Do you live in Jefferson?" she said, wrapping the blanket about the child.

"No. I live in Kinston. I used to—I have practised here, though."

"You have kinfolks here, though. Women. That used to

said. Isom put on the brakes. "I'll get out here and walk," she said.

"You'll do nothing of the kind," Horace said. "Go on, Isom."

"No; wait," the woman said. "We'll be passing people that know you. And then the square."

"Nonsense," Horace said. "Go on, Isom."

"You get out and wait, then," she said. "He can come straight back."

"You'll do no such thing," Horace said. "By heaven, I— Drive on, Isom!"

"You'd better," the woman said. She sat back in the seat. Then she leaned forward again. "Listen. You've been kind. You mean all right, but—"

"You dont think I am lawyer enough, you mean?"

"I guess I've got just what was coming to me. There's no use fighting it."

"Certainly not, if you feel that way about it. But you dont. Or you'd have told Isom to drive you to the railroad station. Wouldn't you?" She was looking down at the child, fretting the blanket about its face. "You get a good night's rest and I'll be in early tomorrow." They passed the jail—a square building slashed harshly by pale slits of light. Only the central window was wide enough to be called a window, criss-crossed by slender bars. In it the Negro murderer leaned; below along the fence a row of heads hatted and bare above work-thickened shoulders, and the blended voices swelled rich and sad into the soft, depthless evening, singing of heaven and being tired. "Dont you worry at all, now. Everybody knows Lee didn't do it."

swift, passing the narrow street. "Here," Horace said, "where are you—" Isom clapped on the brakes.

"Miss Narcissa say to bring you back out home," he said.

"Oh, she did?" Horace said. "That was kind of her. You can tell her I changed her mind."

Isom backed and turned into the narrow street and then into the cedar drive, the lights lifting and boring ahead into the unpruned tunnel as though into the most profound blackness of the sea, as though among straying rigid shapes to which not even light could give color. The car stopped at the door and Horace got out. "You might tell her it was not to her I ran," he said. "Can you remember that?"

Aint no place fer you in whitefolks' jail! Nigger, whar
you gwine to? Whar you gwine to, nigger?"

Each morning Isom fetched in a bottle of milk, which
Horace delivered to the woman at the hotel, for the child.
On Sunday afternoon he went out to his sister's. He left
the woman sitting on the cot in Goodwin's cell, the child
on her lap. Heretofore it had lain in that drugged
apathy, its eyelids closed to thin crescents, but today it
moved now and then in frail, galvanic jerks, whimpering.

Horace went up to Miss Jenny's room. His sister had
not appeared. "He wont talk," Horace said. "He just says
they will have to prove he did it. He said they had nothing on him, no more than on the child. He wouldn't even
consider bond, if he could have got it. He says he is better off in the jail. And I suppose he is. His business out
there is finished now, even if the sheriff hadn't found his
kettles and destroyed—"

"Kettles?"

"His still. After he surrendered, they hunted around
until they found the still. They knew what he was doing,
but they waited until he was down. Then they all jumped
on him. The good customers, that had been buying whiskey from him and drinking all that he would give
them free and maybe trying to make love to his wife behind his back. You should hear them down town. This
morning the Baptist minister took him for a text. Not only
as a murderer, but as an adulterer; a polluter of the free
Democratico-Protestant atmosphere of Yoknapatawpha
county. I gathered that his idea was that Goodwin and
the woman should both be burned as a sole example to
that child; the child to be reared and taught the English

he doesn't . . ." He sat forward, rubbing his hands slowly. "He doesn't realise. . . . Dammit, say what you want to, but there's a corruption about even looking upon evil, even by accident; you cannot haggle, traffic, with putrefaction— You've seen how Narcissa, just hearing about it, how it's made her restless and suspicious. I thought I had come back here of my own accord, but now I see that— Do you suppose she thought I was bringing that woman into the house at night, or something like that?"

"I did too, at first," Miss Jenny said. "But I reckon now she's learned that you'll work harder for whatever reason you think you have, than for anything anybody could offer you or give you."

"You mean, she'd let me think they never had any money, when she—"

"Why not? Aint you doing all right without it?"

Narcissa entered.

"We were just talking about murder and crime," Miss Jenny said.

"I hope you're through, then," Narcissa said. She did not sit down.

"Narcissa has her sorrows too," Miss Jenny said. "Dont you, Narcissa?"

"What now?" Horace said. "She hasn't caught Bory with alcohol on his breath, has she?"

"She's been jilted. Her beau's gone and left her."

"You're such a fool," Narcissa said.

"Yes, sir," Miss Jenny said, "Gowan Stevens has thrown her down. He didn't even come back from that Oxford dance to say goodbye. He just wrote her a letter." She

way in which I can get him out of that jail by tomorrow . . ."

"There's only one way," she said. She looked at him a
moment. Then she turned toward the door. "Which way
did Bory go? Dinner'll be ready soon." She went out.

"And you know what that way is," Miss Jenny said. "If
you aint got any backbone."

"I'll know whether or not I have any backbone when
you tell me what the other way is."

"Go back to Belle," Miss Jenny said. "Go back home."

The Negro murderer was to be hanged on a Saturday
without pomp, buried without circumstance: one night
he would be singing at the barred window and yelling
down out of the soft myriad darkness of a May night;
the next night he would be gone, leaving the window for
Goodwin. Goodwin had been bound over for the June
term of court, without bail. But still he would not agree
to let Horace divulge Popeye's presence at the scene of
the murder.

"I tell you, they've got nothing on me," Goodwin said.

"How do you know they haven't?" Horace said.

"Well, no matter what they think they have on me, I
stand a chance in court. But just let it get to Memphis
that I said he was anywhere around there, what chance
do you think I'd have to get back to this cell after
I testified?"

"You've got the law, justice, civilization."

"Sure, if I spend the rest of my life squatting in that
corner yonder. Come here." He led Horace to the window. "There are five windows in that hotel yonder that

to soothe it, crooning to it, rocking it in her arms. "Maybe
you carry it too much," Horace said; "maybe if you could
leave it at the hotel . . ."

"I guess Lee knows what to do," she said.

"But the lawyer should know all the facts, everything.
He is the one to decide what to tell and what not to tell.
Else, why have one? That's like paying a dentist to fix
your teeth and then refusing to let him look into your
mouth, dont you see? You wouldn't treat a dentist or a
doctor this way." She said nothing, her head bent over
the child. It wailed.

"Hush," she said, "hush, now."

"And worse than that, there's such a thing called ob-
structing justice. Suppose he swears there was nobody
else there, suppose he is about to be cleared—which is
not likely—and somebody turns up who saw Popeye
about the place, or saw his car leaving. Then they'll say,
if Lee didn't tell the truth about an unimportant thing,
why should we believe him when his neck's in danger?"

They reached the hotel. He opened the door for her.
She did not look at him. "I guess Lee knows best," she
said, going in. The child wailed, a thin, whimpering, dis-
tressful cry. "Hush," she said. "Shhhhhhhhhhhh."

Isom had been to fetch Narcissa from a party; it was
late when the car stopped at the corner and picked him
up. A few of the lights were beginning to come on, and
men were already drifting back toward the square after
supper, but it was still too early for the Negro murderer
to begin to sing. "And he'd better sing fast, too," Horace
said. "He's only got two days more." But he was not there
yet. The jail faced west; a last faint copper-colored light

"She say for you to come when you up," the Negro said. "Tell her I'll be there in ten minutes."

As he entered the hotel he passed a young man with a small black bag, such as doctors carry. Horace went on up. The woman was standing in the half-open door, looking down the hall.

"I finally got the doctor," she said. "But I wanted any-way. . . ." The child lay on the bed, its eyes shut, flushed and sweating, its curled hands above its head in the atti-tude of one crucified, breathing in short, whistling gasps. "He was sick all last night. I went and got some medicine and I tried to keep him quiet until daylight. At last I got the doctor." She stood beside the bed, looking down at the child. "There was a woman there," she said. "A young girl."

"A—" Horace said. "Oh," he said. "Yes. You'd better tell me about it."

again in a running popping of cane-stalks like musketry along a trench, without any diminution of speed. Beside the tree Gowan's car lay on its side. Temple looked vaguely and stupidly at it as it too shot behind.

Popeye swung back into the sandy ruts. Yet there was no flight in the action: he performed it with a certain vicious petulance, that was all. It was a powerful car. Even in the sand it held forty miles an hour, and up the narrow gulch to the highroad, where he turned north. Sitting beside him, braced against jolts that had already given way to a smooth increasing hiss of gravel, Temple gazed dully forward as the road she had traversed yesterday began to flee backward under the wheels as onto a spool, feeling her blood seeping slowly inside her loins. She sat limp in the corner of the seat, watching the steady backward rush of the land—pines in opening vistas splashed with fading dogwood; sedge; fields green with new cotton and empty of any movement, peaceful, as though Sunday were a quality of atmosphere, of light and shade—sitting with her legs close together, listening to the hot minute seeping of her blood, saying dully to herself, I'm still bleeding. I'm still bleeding.

It was a bright, soft day, a wanton morning filled with that unbelievable soft radiance of May, rife with a promise of noon and of heat, with high fat clouds like gobs of whipped cream floating lightly as reflections in a mirror, their shadows scudding sedately across the road. It had been a lavender spring. The fruit trees, the white ones, had been in small leaf when the blooms matured; they had never attained that brilliant whiteness of last spring, and the dogwood had come into full bloom after the leaf

"Yes," she whimpered.

"See you do, then. Come on. Get yourself fixed."

She put the compact away. He started the car again.

The road began to thicken with pleasure cars Sunday-bent—small, clay-crusted Fords and Chevrolets; an occasional larger car moving swiftly, with swathed women, and dust-covered hampers; trucks filled with wooden-faced country people in garments like a colored wood meticulously carved; now and then a wagon or a buggy. Before a weathered frame church on a hill the grove was full of tethered teams and battered cars and trucks. The woods gave away to fields; houses became more frequent. Low above the skyline, above roofs and a spire or two, smoke hung. The gravel became asphalt and they entered Dumfries.

Temple began to look about, like one waking from sleep. "Not here!" she said. "I cant—"

"Hush it, now," Popeye said.

"I cant—I might—" she whimpered. "I'm hungry," she said. "I haven't eaten since . . ."

"Ah, you aint hungry. Wait till we get to town."

She looked about with dazed, glassy eyes. "There might be people here . . ." He swung in toward a filling station. "I cant get out," she whimpered. "It's still running, I tell you!"

"Who told you to get out?" He descended and looked at her across the wheel. "Dont you move." She watched him go up the street and enter a door. It was a dingy confectionery. He bought a pack of cigarettes and put one in his mouth. "Gimme a couple of bars of candy," he said. "What kind?"

"Are you coming?" he said. "Are you?"

"I cant. It's down to my stocking now. Look." She lifted her skirt away in a shrinking gesture, then she dropped the skirt and rose again, her torso arching backward, her soundless mouth open as he gripped her. He released her.

"Will you come now?"

She came out from behind the barrel. He took her arm. "It's all over the back of my coat," she whimpered. "Look and see."

"You're all right. I'll get you another coat tomorrow. Come on."

They returned to the car. At the corner she hung back again. "You want some more of it, do you?" he whispered, not touching her. "Do you?" She went on and got in the car quietly. He took the wheel. "Here, I got you a sandwich." He took it from his pocket and put it in her hand. "Come on, now. Eat it." She took a bite obediently. He started the car and took the Memphis road. Again, the bitten sandwich in her hand, she ceased chewing and opened her mouth in that round, hopeless expression of a child; again his hand left the wheel and gripped the back of her neck and she sat motionless, gazing straight at him, her mouth open and the half chewed mass of bread and meat lying upon her tongue.

They reached Memphis in midafternoon. At the foot of the bluff below Main Street Popeye turned into a narrow street of smoke-grimed frame houses with tiers of wooden galleries, set a little back in grassless plots, with now and then a forlorn and hardy tree of some shabby species—gaunt, lopbranched magnolias, a stunted elm or a locust in grayish, cadaverous bloom—interspersed is. Ask any man on the street, cop or not. I've had some of the biggest men in Memphis right here in this house, bankers, lawyers, doctors—all of them. I've had two police captains drinking beer in my dining-room and the commissioner himself upstairs with one of my girls. They got drunk and crashed the door in on him and found him buck-nekkid, dancing the highland fling. A man fifty years old, seven foot tall, with a head like a peanut. He was a fine fellow. He knew me. They all know Reba Rivers. Spent their money here like water, they have. They know me. I aint never double-crossed nobody, honey." She drank beer, breathing thickly into the tankard, the other hand, ringed with yellow diamonds as large as gravel, lost among the lush billows of her breast.

Her slightest movement appeared to be accomplished by an expenditure of breath out of all proportion to any pleasure the movement could afford her. Almost as soon as they entered the house she began to tell Temple about her asthma, toiling up the stairs in front of them, planting her feet heavily in worsted bedroom slippers, a wooden rosary in one hand and the tankard in the other. She had just returned from church, in a black silk gown and a hat savagely flowered; the lower half of the tankard was still frosted with inner chill. She moved heavily from big thigh to thigh, the two dogs moiling underfoot, talking steadily back across her shoulder in a harsh, expiring, maternal voice.

"Popeye knew better than to bring you anywhere else but to my house. I been after him for, how many years I been after you to get you a girl, honey? What I say, a young fellow cant no more live without a girl than . . ."

"Now, now," Miss Reba said. "I bled for four days, my-self. It aint nothing. Doctor Quinn'll stop it in two min-utes, and Minnie'll have them all washed and pressed and you wont never know it. That blood'll be worth a thou-sand dollars to you, honey." She lifted the tankard, the flowers on her hat rigidly moribund, nodding in macabre waes hail. "Us poor girls," she said. The drawn shades, cracked into a myriad pattern like old skin, blew faintly on the bright air, breathing into the room on waning surges the sound of Sabbath traffic, festive, steady, evanes-cent. Temple lay motionless in the bed, her legs straight and close, in covers to her chin and her face small and wan, framed in the rich sprawl of her hair. Miss Reba lowered the tankard, gasping for breath. In her hoarse, fainting voice she began to tell Temple how lucky she was.

"Every girl in the district has been trying to get him, honey. There's one, a little married woman slips down here sometimes, she offered Minnie twenty-five dollars just to get him into the room, that's all. But do you think he'd so much as look at one of them? Girls that have took in a hundred dollars a night. No, sir. Spend his money like water, but do you think he'd look at one of them except to dance with her? I always knowed it wasn't going to be none of these here common whores he'd take. I'd tell them, I'd say, the one of yez that gets him'll wear dia-monds, I says, but it aint going to be none of you com-mon whores, and now Minnie'll have them washed and pressed until you wont know it."

"I cant wear it again," Temple whispered. "I cant."

"No more you'll have to, if you dont want. You can

"Now, now. Now, now. Here, take your drink. This one's on me. I aint going to let no girl of Popeye's—"

"I dont want any more," Temple said.

"Now, now," Miss Reba said. "Drink it and you'll feel better." She lifted Temple's head. Temple clutched the covers to her throat. Miss Reba held the glass to her lips. She gulped it, writhed down again, clutching the covers about her, her eyes wide and black above the covers. "I bet you got that towel disarranged," Miss Reba said, putting her hand on the covers.

"No," Temple whispered. "It's all right. It's still there." She shrank, cringing; they could see the cringing of her legs beneath the covers.

"Did you get Dr Quinn, Minnie?" Miss Reba said.

"Yessum." Minnie was filling the tankard from the bottle, a dull frosting pacing the rise of liquor within the metal. "He say he dont make no Sunday afternoon calls."

"Did you tell him who wanted him? Did you tell him Miss Reba wanted him?"

"Yessum. He say he dont—"

"You go back and tell that suh— You tell him I'll— No; wait." She rose heavily. "Sending a message like that back to me, that can put him in jail three times over." She waddled toward the door, the dogs crowding about the felt slippers. The maid followed and closed the door. Temple could hear Miss Reba cursing the dogs as she descended the stairs with terrific slowness. The sounds died away.

The shades blew steadily in the windows with faint rasping sounds. Temple began to hear a clock. It sat on the mantel above a grate filled with fluted green paper.

"Wait," Temple said. "Let me get back to the bed before Let me get."

"There's a good girl," Miss Reba said. "I knowed she was going to be good."

"Count ten, now," Temple said. "Will you count ten, now?" she said against the wood. She slipped the bolt soundlessly, then she turned and sped back to the bed, her naked feet in pattering diminuendo.

The doctor was a fattish man with thin, curly hair. He wore horn-rimmed glasses which lent to his eyes no distortion at all, as though they were of clear glass and worn for decorum's sake. Temple watched him across the covers, holding them to her throat. "Make them go out," she whispered; "if they'll just go out."

"Now, now," Miss Reba said, "he's going to fix you up." Temple clung to the covers.

"If the little lady will just let . . ." the doctor said. His hair evaporated finely from his brow. His mouth nipped in at the corners, his lips full and wet and red. Behind the glasses his eyes looked like little bicycle wheels at dizzy speed; a metallic hazel. He put out a thick, white hand bearing a masonic ring, haired over with fine reddish fuzz to the second knuckle-joints. Cold air slipped down her body, below her thighs; her eyes were closed. Lying on her back, her legs close together, she began to cry, hopelessly and passively, like a child in a dentist's waiting-room.

"Now, now," Miss Reba said, "take another sup of gin, honey. It'll make you feel better."

the original chaos, and change in turn to a crystal ball holding in its still and cryptic depths the ordered chaos of the intricate and shadowy world upon whose scarred flanks the old wounds whirl onward at dizzy speed into darkness lurking with new disasters.

She was thinking about half-past-ten-oclock. The hour for dressing for a dance, if you were popular enough not to have to be on time. The air would be steamy with re- cent baths, and perhaps powder in the light like chaff in barn-lofts, and they looking at one another, comparing, talking whether you could do more damage if you could just walk out on the floor like you were now. Some wouldn't, mostly ones with short legs. Some of them were all right, but they just wouldn't. They wouldn't say why. The worst one of all said boys thought all girls were ugly except when they were dressed. She said the Snake had been seeing Eve for several days and never noticed her until Adam made her put on a fig leaf. How do you know? they said, and she said because the Snake was there before Adam, because he was the first one thrown out of heaven; he was there all the time. But that wasn't what they meant and they said, How do you know? and Temple thought of her kind of backed up against the dressing table and the rest of them in a circle around her with their combed hair and their shoulders smelling of scented soap and the light powder in the air and their eyes like knives until you could almost watch her flesh where the eyes were touching it, and her eyes in her ugly face courageous and frightened and daring, and they all saying, How do you know? until she told them and held up her hand and swore she had. That was when the other stair and ceased. She listened to the watch. A car started beneath the window with a grind of gears; again the faint bell rang, shrill and prolonged. She found that the faint light yet in the room was from a street lamp. Then she realised that it was night and that the darkness beyond was full of the sound of the city.

She heard the two dogs come up the stairs in a furious scrabble. The noise passed the door and stopped, became utterly still; so still that she could almost see them crouching there in the dark against the wall, watching the stairs. One of them was named Mister something, Temple thought, waiting to hear Miss Reba's feet on the stairs. But it was not Miss Reba; they came too steadily and too lightly. The door opened; the dogs surged in in two shapeless blurs and scuttled under the bed and crouched, whimpering. "You, dawgs!" Minnie's voice said. "You make me spill this." The light came on. Minnie carried a tray. "I got you some supper," she said. "Where them dawgs gone to?"

"Under the bed," Temple said. "I dont want any."

Minnie came and set the tray on the bed and looked down at Temple, her pleasant face knowing and placid. "You want me to—" she said, extending her hand. Temple turned her face quickly away. She heard Minnie kneel, cajoling the dogs, the dogs snarling back at her with whimpering, asthmatic snarls and clicking teeth. "Come outen there, now," Minnie said. "They know fo Miss Reba do when she fixing to get drunk. You, Mr. Binford!"

Temple raised her head. "Mr Binford?"

"He the one with the blue ribbon," Minnie said. Stoop-

nant pool, there seemed to linger spent ghosts of voluptuous gestures and dead lusts. In the corner, upon a faded
scarred strip of oilcloth tacked over the carpet, sat
a washstand bearing a flowered bowl and pitcher and a
row of towels; in the corner behind it sat a slop jar
dressed also in fluted rose-colored paper.

Beneath the bed the dogs made no sound. Temple
moved slightly; the dry complaint of mattress and springs
died into the terrific silence in which they crouched. She
thought of them, woolly, shapeless; savage, petulant,
spoiled, the flatulent monotony of their sheltered lives
snatched up without warning by an incomprehensible
moment of terror and fear of bodily annihilation at the
very hands which symbolised by ordinary the licensed
tranquillity of their lives.

The house was full of sounds. Indistinguishable, remote, they came in to her with a quality of awakening,
resurgence, as though the house itself had been asleep,
rousing itself with dark; she heard something which
might have been a burst of laughter in a shrill woman
voice. Steamy odors from the tray drifted across her face.
She turned her head and looked at it, at the covered and
uncovered dishes of thick china. In the midst of them sat
the glass of pale gin, a pack of cigarettes and a box of
matches. She rose on her elbow, catching up the slipping
gown. She lifted the covers upon a thick steak, potatoes,
green peas; rolls; an anonymous pinkish mass which
some sense—elimination, perhaps—identified as a sweet.
She drew the slipping gown up again, thinking about
them eating down at school in a bright uproar of voices
and clattering forks; of her father and brothers at the sup-

beneath the bed and hurled themselves toward the door in a mad scrabble. As they rushed past her she turned and flung the tankard at them. It struck the door jamb, splashing up the wall, and rebounded with a forlorn clatter. She drew her breath whistling, clutching her breast. She came to the bed and looked down at Temple through the veil. "We was happy as two doves," she wailed, choking, her rings smoldering in hot glints within her billowing breast. "Then he had to go and die on me." She drew her breath whistling, her mouth gaped, shaping the hidden agony of her thwarted lungs, her eyes pale and round with stricken bafflement, protuberant. "As two doves," she roared in a harsh, choking voice.

Again time had overtaken the dead gesture behind the clock crystal: Temple's watch on the table beside the bed said half-past-ten. For two hours she had lain undisturbed, listening. She could distinguish voices now from below stairs. She had been hearing them for some time, lying in the room's musty isolation. Later a mechanical piano began to play. Now and then she heard automobile brakes in the street beneath the window; once two voices quarreling bitterly came up and beneath the shade.

She heard two people—a man and a woman—mount the stairs and enter the room next hers. Then she heard Miss Reba toil up the stairs and pass her door, and lying in the bed, her eyes wide and still, she heard Miss Reba hammering at the next door with the metal tankard and shouting into the wood. Beyond the door the man and woman were utterly quiet, so quiet that Temple thought of the dogs again, thought of them crouching against the began to toss from side to side, opening her mouth to scream. His hand clapped over her mouth, and gripping his wrist, the saliva drooling between his fingers, her body thrashing furiously from thigh to thigh, she saw him crouching beside the bed, his face wrung above his absent chin, his bluish lips protruding as though he were blowing upon hot soup, making a high whinnying sound like a horse. Beyond the wall Miss Reba filled the hall, the house, with a harsh choking uproar of obscene cursing.

neath—and through it Horace could see the courthouse, with men pitching dollars back and forth between holes in the bare earth beneath the locust and water oaks.

The woman brooded above the child. "Nobody wanted her out there. Lee has told them and told them they must not bring women out there, and I told her before it got dark they were not her kind of people and to get away from there. It was that fellow that brought her. He was out there on the porch with them, still drinking, because when he came in to supper he couldn't hardly walk, even. He hadn't even tried to wash the blood off of his face. Little shirt-tail boys that think because Lee breaks the law, they can come out there and treat our house like a . . . Grown people are bad, but at least they take buying whiskey like buying anything else; it's the ones like him, the ones that are too young to realise that people dont break the law just for a holiday." Horace could see her clenched hands writhing in her lap. "God, if I had my way, I'd hang every man that makes it or buys it or drinks it, every one of them.

"But why must it have been me, us? What had I ever done to her, to her kind? I told her to get away from there. I told her not to stay there until dark. But that fellow that brought her was getting drunk again, and him and Van picking at each other. If she'd just stopped running around where they had to look at her. She wouldn't stay anywhere. She'd just dash out one door, and in a minute she'd come running in from the other direction. And if he'd just let Van alone, because Van had to go back on the truck at midnight, and so Popeye would have made him behave. And Saturday night too, choke and catch his breath and moan, sort of, and I would think about that girl lying there in the dark, with her eyes open, listening to them, and me having to stand there, waiting for them to go away so I could do something. I told her to go away. I said 'What fault is it of mine if you're not married? I dont want you here a bit more than you want to be here.' I said 'I've lived my life without any help from people of your sort; what right have you got to look to me for help?' Because I've done everything for him. I've been in the dirt for him. I've put everything behind me and all I asked was to be let alone.

"Then I heard the door open. I could tell Lee by the way he breathes. He went to the bed and said 'I want the raincoat. Sit up and take it off' and I could hear the shucks rattling while he took it off of her, then he went out. He just got the raincoat and went out. It was Van's coat.

"And I have walked around that house so much at night, with those men there, men living off of Lee's risk, men that wouldn't lift a finger for him if he got caught, until I could tell any of them by the way they breathed, and I could tell Popeye by the smell of that stuff on his hair. Tommy was following him. He came in the door behind Popeye and looked at me and I could see his eyes, like a cat. Then his eyes went away and I could feel him sort of squatting against me, and we could hear Popeye over where the bed was and that fellow snoring and snoring.

"I could just hear little faint sounds, from the shucks, so I knew it was all right yet, and in a minute Popeye came on back, and Tommy followed him out, creeping

"He carried a little fool girl out there with him that day and got drunk and ran off and left her. That's what he did. If it hadn't been for that woman— And when I think of people like that walking the earth with impunity just because he has a balloon-tailed suit and went through the astonishing experience of having attended Virginia . . . On any train or in any hotel, on the street; anywhere, mind you—"

"Oh," Miss Jenny said. "I didn't understand at first who you meant. Well," she said. "You remember that last time he was here, just after you came? the day he wouldn't stay for supper and went to Oxford?"

"Yes. And when I think how I could have—"

"He asked Narcissa to marry him. She told him that one child was enough for her."

"I said she has no heart. She cannot be satisfied with less than insult."

"So he got mad and said he would go to Oxford, where there was a woman he was reasonably confident he would not appear ridiculous to: something like that. Well." She looked at him, her neck bowed to see across her spectacles. "I'll declare, a male parent is a funny thing, but just let a man have a hand in the affairs of a female that's no kin to him . . . What is it that makes a man think that the female flesh he marries or begets might misbehave, but all he didn't marry or get is bound to?"

"Yes," Horace said, "and thank God she isn't my flesh and blood. I can reconcile myself to her having to be exposed to a scoundrel now and then, but to think that at any moment she may become involved with a fool."

age with a kind of quiet horror and despair, at a face suddenly older in sin than he would ever be, a face more
blurred than sweet, at eyes more secret than soft. In
reaching for it, he knocked it flat; whereupon once more
the face mused tenderly behind the rigid travesty of the
painted mouth, contemplating something beyond his
shoulder. He lay in bed, dressed, with the light burning,
until he heard the courthouse clock strike three. Then he
left the house, putting his watch and his tobacco pouch
into his pocket.

The railroad station was three quarters of a mile away.
The waiting room was lit by a single weak bulb. It was
empty save for a man in overalls asleep on the bench, his
head on his folded coat, snoring, and a woman in a calico
dress, in a dingy shawl and a new hat trimmed with rigid
and moribund flowers set square and awkward on her
head. Her head was bent; she may have been asleep; her
hands crossed on the paper-wrapped parcel upon her lap,
a straw suit case at her feet. It was then that Horace
found that he had forgot his pipe.

The train came, finding him tramping back and forth
along the cinder-packed right-of-way. The man and
woman got on, the man carrying his rumpled coat, the
woman the parcel and the suit case. He followed them
into the day coach filled with snoring, with bodies
sprawled half into the aisle as though in the aftermath
of a sudden and violent destruction, with dropped
heads, open-mouthed, their throats turned profoundly
upward as though waiting the stroke of knives.

He dozed. The train clicked on, stopped, jolted. He
waked and dozed again. Someone shook him out of sleep

hat, lifting slender hands and preening not-quite-formless fingers about their close heads seen between the sprawled elbows and the leaning heads of two youths hanging over the back of the seat and surrounded by colored hat bands at various heights where the owners sat on the seat arms or stood in the aisle; and presently the conductor's cap as he thrust among them with plaintive, fretful cries, like a bird.

"Tickets. Tickets, please," he chanted. For an instant they held him there, invisible save for his cap. Then two young men slipped swiftly back and into the seat behind Horace. He could hear them breathing. Forward the conductor's punch clicked twice. He came on back. "Tickets," he chanted. "Tickets." He took Horace's and stopped where the youths sat.

"You already got mine," one said. "Up there."

"Where's your check?" the conductor said.

"You never gave us any. You got our tickets, though. Mine was number—" he repeated a number glibly, in a frank, pleasant tone. "Did you notice the number of yours, Shack?"

The second one repeated a number in a frank, pleasant tone. "Sure you got ours. Look and see." He began to whistle between his teeth, a broken dance rhythm, unmusical.

"Do you eat at Gordon hall?" the other said.

"No. I have natural halitosis." The conductor went on. The whistle reached crescendo, clapped off by his hands on his knees, ejaculating duh-duh-duh. Then he just squalled, meaningless, vertiginous; to Horace it was like sitting before a series of printed pages turned in furious

At the top of the hill three paths diverged through a broad grove beyond which, in green vistas, buildings in red brick or gray stone gleamed, and where a clear soprano bell began to ring. The procession became three streams, thinning rapidly upon the dawdling couples, swinging hands, strolling in erratic surges, lurching into one another with puppyish squeals, with the random intense purposelessness of children.

The broader path led to the postoffice. He entered and waited until the window was clear.

"I'm trying to find a young lady, Miss Temple Drake. I probably just missed her, didn't I?"

"She's not here any longer," the clerk said. "She quit school about two weeks ago." He was young: a dull, smooth face behind horn glasses, the hair meticulous. After a time Horace heard himself asking quietly:

"You dont know where she went?"

The clerk looked at him. He leaned, lowering his voice: "Are you another detective?"

"Yes," Horace said, "yes. No matter. It doesn't matter." Then he was walking quietly down the steps, into the sunlight again. He stood there while on both sides of him they passed in a steady stream of little colored dresses, bare-armed, with close bright heads, with that identical cool, innocent, unabashed expression which he knew well in their eyes, above the savage identical paint upon their mouths; like music moving, like honey poured in sunlight, pagan and evanescent and serene, thinly evocative of all lost days and outpaced delights, in the sun. Bright, trembling with heat, it lay in open glades of miragelike glimpses of stone or brick: columns without tops, towers on, swaying on the curves, flashing past an occasional house, through cuts and across valleys where young cotton wheeled slowly in fanlike rows.

The train checked speed; a jerk came back, and four whistle-blasts. The man in the soiled hat entered, taking a cigar from his breast pocket. He came down the aisle swiftly, looking at Horace. He slowed, the cigar in his fingers. The train jolted again. The man flung his hand out and caught the back of the seat facing Horace.

"Aint this Judge Benbow?" he said. Horace looked up into a vast, puffy face without any mark of age or thought whatever—a majestic sweep of flesh on either side of a small blunt nose, like looking out over a mesa, yet withal some indefinable quality of delicate paradox, as though the Creator had completed his joke by lighting the munificent expenditure of putty with something orig- inally intended for some weak, acquisitive creature like a squirrel or a rat. "Dont I address Judge Benbow?" he said, offering his hand. "I'm Senator Snopes, Cla'ence Snopes."

"Oh," Horace said, "yes. Thanks," he said, "but I'm afraid you anticipate a little. Hope, rather."

The other waved the cigar, the other hand, palm-up, the third finger discolored faintly at the base of a huge ring, in Horace's face. Horace shook it and freed his hand. "I thought I recognised you when you got on at Oxford," Snopes said, "but I— May I set down?" he said, already shoving at Horace's knee with his leg. He flung the over- coat—a shoddy blue garment with a greasy velvet col- lar—on the seat and sat down as the train stopped. "Yes, sir, I'm always glad to see any of the boys, any time . . ."

"You can smoke here. There aren't any ladies."

"Sure," Snopes said. "I'll see you at Holly Springs." He went on back toward the day coach and passed out of sight with the cigar in his mouth. Horace remembered him ten years ago as a hulking, dull youth, son of a restaurant-owner, member of a family which had been moving from the Frenchman's Bend neighborhood into Jefferson for the past twenty years, in sections; a family of enough ramifications to have elected him to the legislature without recourse to a public polling.

He sat quite still, the cold pipe in his hand. He rose and went forward through the day coach, then into the smoker. Snopes was in the aisle, his thigh draped over the arm of a seat where four men sat, using the unlighted cigar to gesture with. Horace caught his eye and beckoned from the vestibule. A moment later Snopes joined him, the overcoat on his arm.

"How are things going at the capital?" Horace said.

Snopes began to speak in his harsh, assertive voice. There emerged gradually a picture of stupid chicanery and petty corruption for stupid and petty ends, conducted principally in hotel rooms into which bellboys whisked with bulging jackets upon discreet flicks of skirts in swift closet doors. "Any time you're in town," he said. "I always like to show the boys around. Ask anybody in town; they'll tell you if it's there, Cla'ence Snopes'll know where it is. You got a pretty tough case up home there, what I hear."

"Cant tell yet," Horace said. He said: "I stopped off at Oxford today, at the university, speaking to some of my step-daughter's friends. One of her best friends is no the vestibule, then he stepped quickly back into the car. Snopes emerged from the day coach as the porter opened the door and swung down the step, stool in hand. Snopes descended. He took something from his breast pocket and gave it to the porter. "Here, George," he said, "have a cigar."

Horace descended. Snopes went on, the soiled hat towering half a head above any other. Horace looked at the porter.

"He gave it to you, did he?"

The porter chucked the cigar on his palm. He put it in his pocket.

"What're you going to do with it?" Horace said.

"I wouldn't give it to nobody I know," the porter said.

"Does he do this very often?"

"Three-four times a year. Seems like I always git him, too . . . Thank' suh."

Horace saw Snopes enter the waiting-room; the soiled hat, the vast neck, passed again out of his mind. He filled the pipe again.

From a block away he heard the Memphis-bound train come in. It was at the platform when he reached the station. Beside the open vestibule Snopes stood, talking with two youths in new straw hats, with something vaguely mentorial about his thick shoulders and his gestures. The train whistled. The two youths got on. Horace stepped back around the corner of the station.

When his train came he saw Snopes get on ahead of him and enter the smoker. Horace knocked out his pipe and entered the day coach and found a seat at the rear, facing backward.

vest open upon a neat paunch. The woman was not there. "It's these church ladies," he said. He lowered his voice, the toothpick in his fingers. "They come in this morning. A committee of them. You know how it is, I reckon."

"You mean to say you let the Baptist church dictate who your guests shall be?"

"It's them ladies. You know how it is, once they get set on a thing. A man might just as well give up and do like they say. Of course, with me—"

"By God, if there was a man—"

"Shhhhhh," the proprietor said. "You know how it is when them—"

"But of course there wasn't a man who would— And you call yourself one, that'll let—"

"I got a certain position to keep up myself," the proprietor said in a placative tone. "If you come right down to it." He stepped back a little, against the desk. "I reckon I can say who'll stay in my house and who wont," he said. "And I know some more folks around here that better do the same thing. Not no mile off, neither. I aint beholden to no man. Not to you, noways."

"Where is she now? or did they drive her out of town?"

"That aint my affair, where folks go after they check out," the proprietor said, turning his back. He said: "I reckon somebody took her in, though."

"Yes," Horace said. "Christians. Christians." He turned toward the door. The proprietor called him. He turned. The other was taking a paper down from a pigeon-hole. Horace returned to the desk. The paper lay on the desk. The proprietor leaned with his hands on the desk, the toothpick tilted in his mouth.

she has been practically turned into the streets? That—"

"That shouldn't be a hardship. She ought to be used to that."

He looked at her. He put the pipe in his mouth and smoked it to a careful coal, watching his hand tremble upon the stem. "Listen. By tomorrow they will probably ask her to leave town. Just because she happens not to be married to the man whose child she carries about these sanctified streets. But who told them? That's what I want to know. I know that nobody in Jefferson knew it except—"

"You were the first I heard tell it," Miss Jenny said. "But, Narcissa, why—"

"Not in my house," Narcissa said.

"Well," Horace said. He drew the pipe to an even coal. "That settles it, of course," he said, in a dry, light voice. She rose. "Will you stay here tonight?"

"What? No. No. I'll—I told her I'd come for her at the jail and . . ." He sucked at his pipe. "Well, I don't suppose it matters. I hope it doesn't."

She was still paused, turning. "Will you stay or not?"

"I could even tell her I had a puncture," Horace said. "Time's not such a bad thing after all. Use it right, and you can stretch anything out, like a rubberband, until it busts somewhere, and there you are, with all tragedy and despair in two little knots between thumb and finger of each hand."

"Will you stay, or wont you stay, Horace?" Narcissa said.

"I think I'll stay," Horace said.

He was in bed. He had been lying in the dark for about

"I dont think anything about it. I don't care. That's what people in town think. So it doesn't matter whether it's true or not. What I do mind is, every day you force me to have to tell lies for you. Go away from here, Horace. Anybody but you would realise it's a case of cold-blooded murder."

"And over her, of course. I suppose they say that too, out of their odorous and omnipotent sanctity. Do they say yet that it was I killed him?"

"I dont see that it makes any difference who did it. The question is, are you going to stay mixed up with it? When people already believe you and she are slipping into my house at night." Her cold, unbending voice shaped the words in the darkness above him. Through the window, upon the blowing darkness, came the drowsy dissonance of cicada and cricket.

"Do you believe that?" he said.

"It doesn't matter what I believe. Go on away, Horace. I ask it."

"And leave her—them, flat?"

"Hire a lawyer, if he still insists he's innocent. I'll pay for it. You can get a better criminal lawyer than you are. She wont know it. She wont even care. Cant you see that she is just leading you on to get him out of jail for nothing? Dont you know that woman has got money hidden away somewhere? You're going back into town tomorrow, are you?" She turned, began to dissolve into the blackness. "You wont leave before breakfast."

The next morning at breakfast, his sister said: "Who will be the lawyer on the other side of the case?"

always say—" he leaned, his voice lowered, his mud-col-
ored eyes roving aside "—the church aint got no place in
politics, and women aint got no place in neither one, let
alone the law. Let them stay at home and they'll
find plenty to do without upsetting a man's law-suit. And
besides, a man aint no more than human, and what he
does aint nobody's business but his. What you done with
her?"

"She's at the jail," Horace said. He spoke shortly, making to pass on. The other blocked his way with an effect
of clumsy accident.

"You got them all stirred up, anyhow. Folks is saying
you wouldn't git Goodwin no bond, so he'd have to
stay—" again Horace made to pass on. "Half the trouble
in this world is caused by women, I always say. Like that
girl gittin her paw all stirred up, running off like she
done. I reckon he done the right thing sending her clean
outen the state."

"Yes," Horace said in a dry, furious voice.

"I'm mighty glad to hear your case is going all right.
Between you and me, I'd like to see a good lawyer make
a monkey outen that District Attorney. Give a fellow
like that a little county office and he gits too big for his
pants right away. Well, glad to've saw you. I got some
business up town for a day or two. I dont reckon you'll be
going up that-a-way?"

"What?" Horace said. "Up where?"

"Memphis. Anything I can do for you?"

"No," Horace said. He went on. For a short distance he
could not see at all. He tramped steadily, the muscles
beside his jaws beginning to ache, passing people who
spoke to him, unawares.

Fonzo was watching him, his blue eyes like china. "What's the matter with you? All the time on the train you was talking about how many times you been to Memphis. I bet you aint never bu—" Someone jostled them, thrust them apart; a stream of people began to flow between them. Clutching his suit case and hat Fonzo fought his way back to his friend.

"I have, too," Virgil said, looking glassily about.

"Well, what we going to do then? It wont be open till eight oclock in the morning."

"What you in such a rush for, then?"

"Well, I dont aim to stay here all night. . . . What did you do when you was here before?"

"Went to the hotel," Virgil said.

"Which one? They got more than one here. You reckon all these folks could stay in one hotel? Which one was it?"

Virgil's eyes were also a pale, false blue. He looked glassily about. "The Gayoso hotel," he said.

"Well, let's go to it," Fonzo said. They moved toward the exit. A man shouted "taxi" at them; a redcap tried to take Fonzo's bag. "Look out," he said, drawing it back. On the street more cabmen barked at them.

"So this is Memphis," Fonzo said. "Which way is it, now?" He had no answer. He looked around and saw Virgil in the act of turning away from a cabman. "What you—"

"Up this way," Virgil said. "It aint far."

It was a mile and a half. From time to time they swapped hands with the bags. "So this is Memphis," Fonzo said. "Where have I been all my life?" When they entrance a lattice-work false entry leaned. On the steps sat a big woman in a mother hubbard, watching two fluffy white dogs which moved about the yard.

"Let's try that un," Fonzo said.

"That aint no hotel. Where's ere sign?"

"Why aint it?" Fonzo said. "'Course it is. Who ever heard of anybody just living in a three-storey house?"

"We cant go in this-a-way," Virgil said. "This hyer's the back. Dont you see that privy?" jerking his head toward the lattice.

"Well, let's go around to the front, then," Fonzo said. "Come on."

They went around the block. The opposite side was filled by a row of automobile salesrooms. They stood in the middle of the block, their suit cases in their right hands.

"I dont believe you was ever here before, noways," Fonzo said.

"Let's go back. That must a been the front."

"With the privy built onto the front door?" Fonzo said.

"We can ask that lady."

"Who can? I aint."

"Let's go back and see, anyway."

They returned. The woman and the dogs were gone.

"Now you done it," Fonzo said. "Aint you?"

"Let's wait a while. Maybe she'll come back."

"It's almost seven oclock," Fonzo said.

They set the bags down beside the fence. The lights had come on, quivering high in the serried windows against the tall serene western sky.

"I can smell ham, too," Fonzo said.

"If it aint too high," Virgil said.

Miss Reba looked at him. "Where you from, honey?"

They told her, and their names. "We aim to be hyer a month or more, if it suits us."

"Why, I reckon so," she said after a while. She looked at them. "I can let you have a room, but I'll have to charge you extra whenever you do business in it. I got my living to make like everybody else."

"We aint," Fonzo said. "We'll do our business at the college."

"What college?" Miss Reba said.

"The barber's college," Fonzo said.

"Look here," Miss Reba said, "you little whipper-snapper." Then she began to laugh, her hand at her breast. They watched her soberly while she laughed in harsh gasps. "Lord, Lord," she said. "Come in here."

The room was at the top of the house, at the back. Miss Reba showed them the bath. When she put her hand on the door a woman's voice said: "Just a minute, dearie" and the door opened and she passed them, in a kimono. They watched her go up the hall, rocked a little to their young foundations by a trail of scent which she left. Fonzo nudged Virgil surreptitiously. In their room again he said:

"That was another one. She's got two daughters. Hold me, big boy; I'm heading for the henhouse."

They didn't go to sleep for some time that first night, what with the strange bed and room and the voices. They could hear the city, evocative and strange, imminent and remote; threat and promise both—a deep, steady sound upon which invisible lights glittered and

"Dont know," Virgil said.

"Wish I worked for her, anyway," Fonzo said. "With all them women in kimonos and such running around."

"Wouldn't do you no good," Virgil said. "They're all married. Aint you heard them?"

The next afternoon when they returned from the school they found a woman's undergarment under the washstand . . . Fonzo picked it up. "She's a dress-maker," he said.

"Reckon so," Virgil said. "Look and see if they taken anything of yourn."

The house appeared to be filled with people who did not sleep at night at all. They could hear them at all hours, running up and down the stairs, and always Fonzo would be conscious of women, of female flesh. It got to where he seemed to lie in his celibate bed sur-rounded by women, and he would lie beside the steadily snoring Virgil, his ears strained for the murmurs, the whispers of silk that came through the walls and the floor, that seemed to be as much a part of both as the planks and the plaster, thinking that he had been in Memphis ten days, yet the extent of his acquaintance was a few of his fellow pupils at the school. After Virgil was asleep he would rise and unlock the door and leave it ajar, but nothing happened.

On the twelfth day he told Virgil they were going visiting, with one of the barber-students.

"Where?" Virgil said.

"That's all right. You come on. I done found out some-thing. And when I think I been here two weeks without knowing about it—"

"You made me spend three dollars," Virgil said.

"Aw, shut up," Fonzo said. "When I think I been here for two whole weeks almost . . ."

The next afternoon they came home through the dusk, with the lights winking on, beginning to flare and gleam, and the women on their twinkling blonde legs meeting men and getting into automobiles and such.

"How about that three dollars now?" Fonzo said.

"I reckon we better not go over tonight," Virgil said. "It'll cost too much."

"That's right," Fonzo said. "Somebody might see us and tell her."

They waited two nights. "Now it'll be six dollars," Virgil said.

"Dont come, then," Fonzo said.

When they returned home Fonzo said: "Try to act like something, this time. She near about caught us before on account of the way you acted."

"What if she does?" Virgil said in a sullen voice. "She caint eat us."

They stood outside the lattice, whispering.

"How you know she caint?" Fonzo said.

"She dont want to, then."

"How you know she dont want to?"

"Maybe she dont," Virgil said. Fonzo opened the lattice door. "I caint eat that six dollars, noways," Virgil said. "Wisht I could."

Minnie let them in. She said: "Somebody huntin you all." They waited in the hall.

"We done caught now," Virgil said. "I told you about throwing that money away."

XXii

ON THE THIRD DAY of his search, Horace found a domi-
cile for the woman and child. It was in the ramshackle
house of an old half-crazed white woman who was believed to manufacture spells for Negroes. It was on the
edge of town, set in a tiny plot of ground choked and
massed with waist-high herbage in an unbroken jungle
across the front. At the back a path had been trodden
from the broken gate to the door. All night a dim light
burned in the crazy depths of the house and at almost
any hour of the twenty-four a wagon or a buggy might
be seen tethered in the lane behind it and a Negro entering or leaving the back door.

The house had been entered once by officers searching
for whiskey. They found nothing save a few dried
bunches of weeds, and a collection of dirty bottles con-
taining liquid of which they could say nothing surely
save that it was not alcoholic, while the old woman, held
by two men, her lank grayish hair shaken before the glit-

"This is Snopes," it said. "How're you, Judge?"

"What?" Horace said. "Who is it?"

"Senator Snopes, Cla'ence Snopes." The victrola blared, faint, far away; he could see the man, the soiled hat, the thick shoulders, leaning above the instrument—in a drugstore or a restaurant—whispering into it behind a soft, huge, ringed hand, the telephone toylike in the other.

"Oh," Horace said. "Yes? What is it?"

"I got a little piece of information that might interest you."

"Information that would interest me?"

"I reckon so. That would interest a couple of parties." Against Horace's ear the radio or the victrola performed a reedy arpeggio of saxophones. Obscene, facile, they seemed to be quarreling with one another like two dextrous monkeys in a cage. He could hear the gross breathing of the man at the other end of the wire.

"All right," he said. "What do you know that would interest me?"

"I'll let you judge that."

"All right. I'll be down town in the morning. You can find me somewhere." Then he said immediately: "Hello!" The man sounded as though he were breathing in Horace's ear: a placid, gross sound, suddenly portentous somehow. "Hello!" Horace said.

"It evidently dont interest you, then. I reckon I'll dicker with the other party and not trouble you no more. Goodbye."

"No; wait," Horace said. "Hello! Hello!"

"Yeuh?"

that, striking always that vast, soft, inert bulk, as though it were caught in an avalanche of cottonseed-hulls.

"Let's go to the house," Horace said. Snopes opened the door. "Go on," Horace said, "I'll walk up." Snopes drove on. He was getting out of the car when Horace overtook him. "Well, what is it?" Horace said.

Again Snopes looked at the house. "Keeping batch, are you?" he said. Horace said nothing. "Like I always say, every married man ought to have a little place of his own, where he can git off to himself without it being nobody's business what he does. 'Course a man owes something to his wife, but what they dont know caint hurt them, does it? Long's he does that, I caint see where she's got ere kick coming. Aint that what you say?"

"She's not here," Horace said, "if that's what you're hinting it. What did you want to see me about?"

Again he felt Snopes watching him, the unabashed stare calculating and completely unbelieving. "Well, I always say, caint nobody tend to a man's private busi-ness but himself. I aint blaming you. But when you know me better, you'll know I aint loose-mouthed. I been around. I been there. . . . Have a cigar?" His big hand flicked to his breast and offered two cigars.

"No, thanks."

Snopes lit a cigar, his face coming out of the match like a pie set on edge.

"What did you want to see me about?" Horace said.

Snopes puffed the cigar. "Couple days ago I come onto a piece of information which will be of value to you, if I aint mistook."

"Oh. Of value. What value?"

course, if it dont, I'll dicker with the other party. I just give you the chance."

Horace turned toward the steps. He moved gingerly, like an old man. "Let's sit down," he said. Snopes followed and sat on the step. They sat in the moonlight. "You know where she is?"

"I seen her." Again he drew his hand across the back of his neck. "Yes, sir. If she aint—hasn't been there, you can git your money back. I caint say no fairer, can I?"

"And what's your price?" Horace said. Snopes puffed the cigar to a careful coal. "Go on," Horace said. "I'm not going to haggle." Snopes told him. "All right," Horace said. "I'll pay it." He drew his knees up and set his elbows on them and laid his hands to his face. "Where is— Wait. Are you a Baptist, by any chance?"

"My folks is. I'm putty liberal, myself. I aint hidebound in no sense, as you'll find when you know me better."

"All right," Horace said from behind his hands. "Where is she?"

"I'll trust you," Snopes said. "She's in a Memphis 'ho'-house."

telling what we know, caint none of us git off a train at Jefferson again, hey?"

"You know as well as I do what I'm doing here. What do you want with me?"

"Sure; sure," Snopes said. "I know how a feller feels, married and all and not being sho where his wife is at." Between jerky glances over his shoulder he winked at Horace. "Make your mind easy. It's the same with me as if the grave knowed it. Only I hate to see a good—" Horace had gone on toward the door. "Judge," Snopes said in a penetrant undertone. Horace turned. "Dont stay."

"Dont stay?"

"See her and then leave. It's a sucker place. Place for farm-boys. Higher'n Monte Carlo. I'll wait out hyer and I'll show you a place where—" Horace went on and entered the lattice. Two hours later, as he sat talking to Miss Reba in her room while beyond the door feet and now and then voices came and went in the hall and on the stair, Minnie entered with a torn scrap of paper and brought it to Horace.

"What's that?" Miss Reba said.

"That big pie-face-ted man left it fer him," Minnie said. "He say fer you to come on down there."

"Did you let him in?" Miss Reba said.

"Nome. He never tried to git in."

"I guess not," Miss Reba said. She grunted. "Do you know him?" she said to Horace.

"Yes. I cant seem to help myself," Horace said. He opened the paper. Torn from a handbill, it bore an address in pencil in a neat, flowing hand.

nuttin except to get out and stay out, see; so this day it's about two in the afternoon and I'm asleep and Minnie lets him in and he asks her who's here and she tells him aint nobody, and he goes on up stairs. And Minnie says about that time Popeye comes in. She says she dont know what to do. She's scared not to let him in, and she says she knows if she does and he spatters that big bastard all over the upstairs floor, she knows I'll fire her and her husband just quit her and all.

"So Popeye goes on upstairs on them cat feet of his and comes on your friend on his knees, peeping through the keyhole. Minnie says Popeye stood behind him for about a minute, with his hat cocked over one eye. She says he took out a cigarette and struck a match on his thumbnail without no noise and lit it and then she says he reached over and held the match to the back of your friend's neck, and Minnie says she stood there halfway up the stairs and watched them: that fellow kneeling there with his face like a pie took out of the oven too soon and Popeye squirting smoke through his nose and kind of jerking his head at him. Then she come on down and in about ten seconds here he comes down the stairs with both hands on top of his head, going wump-wump-wump inside like one of these here big dray-horses, and he pawed at the door for about a minute, moaning to himself like the wind in a chimney Minnie says, until she opened the door and let him out. And that's the last time he's even rung this bell until tonight. . . . Let me see that." Horace gave her the paper. "That's a nigger whore-house," she said. "The lous— Minnie, tell him his friend aint here. Tell him I dont know where he went."

breath. She put her hand on his head and tilted his face up. "You aint lying to me, are you?" she said, her eyes piercing and intent and sad. "No, you aint." She released him. "Wait here a minute. I'll see." She went out. He heard her speak to Minnie in the hall, then he heard her toil up the stairs.

He sat quietly as she had left him. The room contained a wooden bed, a painted screen, three over-stuffed chairs, a wall safe. The dressing-table was littered with toilet articles tied in pink satin bows. The mantel supported a wax lily beneath a glass bell; above it, draped in black, the photograph of a meek-looking man with an enormous moustache. On the walls hung a few lithographs of spurious Greek scenes, and one picture done in tatting. Horace rose and went to the door. Minnie sat in a chair in the dim hall.

"Minnie," he said, "I've got to have a drink. A big one." He had just finished it when Minnie entered again. "She say fer you to come on up," she said.

He mounted the stairs. Miss Reba waited at the top. She led the way up the hall and opened a door into a dark room. "You'll have to talk to her in the dark," she said. "She wont have no light." Light from the hall fell through the door and across the bed. "This aint hers," Miss Reba said. "Wouldn't even see you in her room at all. I reckon you better humor her until you find out what you want." They entered. The light fell across the bed, upon a motionless curving ridge of bedclothing, the general tone of the bed unbroken. She'll smother, Horace thought. "Honey," Miss Reba said. The ridge did not move. "Here he is, honey. Long as you're all covered send for you. You and him dont want to stay here in Memphis. The lawyer'll take care of you and you wont have to tell nuttin you—" The ridge moved. Temple flung the covers back and sat up. Her head was tousled, her face puffed, two spots of rouge on her cheekbones and her mouth painted into a savage cupid's bow. She stared for an instant at Horace with black antagonism, then she looked away.

"I want a drink," she said, pulling up the shoulder of her gown.

"Lie down," Miss Reba said. "You'll catch cold."

"I want another drink," Temple said.

"Lie down and cover up your nekkidness, anyway," Miss Reba said, rising. "You already had three since supper."

Temple dragged the gown up again. She looked at Horace. "You give me a drink, then."

"Come on, honey," Miss Reba said, trying to push her down. "Lie down and get covered up and tell him about that business. I'll get you a drink in a minute."

"Let me alone," Temple said, writhing free. Miss Reba drew the covers about her shoulders. "Give me a cigarette, then. Have you got one?" she asked Horace.

"I'll get you one in a minute," Miss Reba said. "Will you do what he wants you to?"

"What?" Temple said. She looked at Horace with her black, belligerent stare.

"You needn't tell me where your—he—" Horace said.

"Dont think I'm afraid to tell," Temple said. "I'll tell it anywhere. Dont think I'm afraid. I want a drink."

of the stage; suddenly Horace realised that she was re-counting the experience with actual pride, a sort of naïve and impersonal vanity, as though she were making it up, looking from him to Miss Reba with quick, darting glances like a dog driving two cattle along a lane.

"And so whenever I breathed I'd hear those shucks. I dont see how anybody ever sleeps on a bed like that. But maybe you get used to it. Or maybe they're tired at night. Because when I breathed I could hear them, even when I was just sitting on the bed. I didn't see how it could be just breathing, so I'd sit as still as I could, but I could still hear them. That's because breathing goes down. You think it goes up, but it doesn't. It goes down you, and I'd hear them getting drunk on the porch. I got to thinking I could see where their heads were leaning back against the wall and I'd say Now this one's drinking out of the jug. Now that one's drinking. Like the mashed-in place on the pillow after you got up, you know.

"That was when I got to thinking a funny thing. You know how you do when you're scared. I was looking at my legs and I'd try to make like I was a boy. I was think-ing about if I just was a boy and then I tried to make myself into one by thinking. You know how you do things like that. Like when you know one problem in class and when they came to that you look at him and think right hard, Call on me. Call on me. Call on me. I'd think about what they tell children, about kissing your elbow, and I tried to. I actually did. I was that scared, and I'd wonder if I could tell when it happened. I mean, before I looked, and I'd think I had and how I'd go out and show them—you know. I'd strike a match and say him and I'd think about the blood running on me and how I'd say I guess that'll teach you! I guess you'll let me alone now! I'd say. I didn't know it was going to be just the other way . . . I want a drink."

"I'll get you one in a minute," Miss Reba said. "Go on and tell him."

"Oh, yes; this was something else funny I did." She told about lying in the darkness with Gowan snoring beside her, listening to the shucks and hearing the darkness full of movement, feeling Popeye approaching. She could hear the blood in her veins, and the little muscles at the corners of her eyes cracking faintly wider and wider, and she could feel her nostrils going alternately cool and warm. Then he was standing over and she was saying Come on. Touch me. Touch me! You're a coward if you dont. Coward! Coward!

"I wanted to go to sleep, you see. And he just kept on standing there. I thought if he'd just go on and get it over with, I could go to sleep. So I'd say You're a coward if you dont! You're a coward if you dont! and I could feel my mouth getting fixed to scream, and that little hot ball inside you that screams. Then it touched me, that nasty little cold hand, fiddling around inside the coat where I was naked. It was like alive ice and my skin started jumping away from it like those little flying fish in front of a boat. It was like my skin knew which way it was going to go before it started moving, and my skin would keep on jerking just ahead of it like there wouldn't be anything there when the hand got there.

"Then it got down to where my insides begin, and I hadn't eaten since yesterday at dinner and my insides

"Then I said That wont do. I ought to be a man. So I was an old man, with a long white beard, and then the little black man got littler and littler and I was saying Now. You see now. I'm a man now. Then I thought about being a man, and as soon as I thought it, it happened. It made a kind of plopping sound, like blowing a little rubber tube wrong-side outward. It felt cold, like the inside of your mouth when you hold it open. I could feel it, and I lay right still to keep from laughing about how surprised he was going to be. I could feel the jerking going on inside my knickers ahead of his hand and me lying there trying not to laugh about how surprised and mad he was going to be in about a minute. Then all of a sudden I went to sleep. I couldn't even stay awake until his hand got there. I just went to sleep. I couldn't even feel myself jerking in front of his hand, but I could hear the shucks. I didn't wake up until that woman came and took me down to the crib."

As he was leaving the house Miss Reba said: "I wish you'd get her down there and not let her come back. I'd find her folks myself, if I knowed how to go about it. But you know how . . . She'll be dead, or in the asylum in a year, way him and her go on up there in that room. There's something funny about it that I aint found out about yet. Maybe it's her. She wasn't born for this kind of life. You have to be born for this like you have to be born a butcher or a barber, I guess. Wouldn't anybody be either of them just for money or fun."

Better for her if she were dead tonight, Horace thought, walking on. For me, too. He thought of her, Popeye, the woman, the child, Goodwin, all put into a filled with all the nightmare shapes it had taken him forty-three years to invent, concentrated in a hot, hard lump in his stomach. Suddenly he was walking fast, the coffee jolting like a hot, heavy rock inside him.

He walked quietly up the drive, beginning to smell the honeysuckle from the fence. The house was dark, still, as though it were marooned in space by the ebb of all time. The insects had fallen to a low monotonous pitch, everywhere, nowhere, spent, as though the sound were the chemical agony of a world left stark and dying above the tide-edge of the fluid in which it lived and breathed. The moon stood overhead, but without light; the earth lay beneath, without darkness. He opened the door and felt his way into the room and to the light. The voice of the night—insects, whatever it was—had followed him into the house; he knew suddenly that it was the friction of the earth on its axis, approaching that moment when it must decide to turn on or to remain forever still: a motionless ball in cooling space, across which a thick smell of honeysuckle writhed like cold smoke.

He found the light and turned it on. The photograph sat on the dresser. He took it up, holding it in his hands. Enclosed by the narrow imprint of the missing frame Little Belle's face dreamed with that quality of sweet chiaroscuro. Communicated to the cardboard by some quality of the light or perhaps by some infinitesimal movement of his hands, his own breathing, the face appeared to breathe in his palms in a shallow bath of highlight, beneath the slow, smokelike tongues of invisible honeysuckle. Almost palpable enough to be seen, the scent filled the room and the small face seemed to swoon

XXIV

THE FIRST TIME Temple went to the head of the stairs Minnie's eyeballs rolled out of the dusky light beside Miss Reba's door. Leaning once more within her bolted door Temple heard Miss Reba toil up the stairs and knock. Temple leaned silently against the door while Miss Reba panted and wheezed beyond it with a mixture of blandishment and threat. She made no sound. After a while Miss Reba went back down the stairs.

Temple turned from the door and stood in the center of the room, beating her hands silently together, her eyes black in her livid face. She wore a street dress, a hat. She removed the hat and hurled it into a corner and went and flung herself face down upon the bed. The bed had not been made. The table beside it was littered with cigarette stubs, the adjacent floor strewn with ashes. The pillow slip on that side was spotted with brown holes. Often in the night she would wake to smell tobacco and

and lay again on her face in a slow thickening of expensive scent.

At noon Minnie tapped at the door. "Here yo dinner." Temple didn't move. "I ghy leave it here by the door. You can git it when you wants it." Her feet went away. Temple did not move.

Slowly the bar of sunlight shifted across the floor; the western side of the window-frame was now in shadow. Temple sat up, her head turned aside as though she were listening, fingering with deft habitude at her hair. She rose quietly and went to the door and listened again. Then she opened it. The tray sat on the floor. She stepped over it and went to the stairs and peered over the rail. After a while she made Minnie out, sitting in a chair in the hall.

"Minnie," she said. Minnie's head jerked up; again her eyes rolled whitely. "Bring me a drink," Temple said. She returned to her room. She waited fifteen minutes. She banged the door and was tramping furiously down the stairs when Minnie appeared in the hall.

"Yessum," Minnie said, "Miss Reba say— We aint got no—" Miss Reba's door opened. Without looking up at Temple she spoke to Minnie. Minnie lifted her voice again. "Yessum; all right. I bring it up in just a minute."

"You'd better," Temple said. She returned and stood just inside the door until she heard Minnie mount the stairs. Temple opened the door, holding it just ajar.

"Aint you going to eat no dinner?" Minnie said, thrusting at the door with her knee. Temple held it to.

"Where is it?" she said.

Temple opened the lattice and peered out. The street was empty save for a taxi at the curb across the way, and a man in a cap standing in a door beyond it. She went down the street, walking swiftly. At the corner a cab overtook her, slowing, the driver looking at her interrogatively. She turned into the drug store at the corner and went back to the telephone booth. Then she returned to the house. As she turned the corner she met the man in the cap who had been leaning in the door. She entered the lattice. Minnie opened the door.

"Thank goodness," Minnie said. "When that cab over there started up, I got ready to pack up too. If you aint ghy say nothing about it, I git you a drink."

When Minnie fetched the gin Temple started to drink it. Her hand was trembling and there was a sort of elation in her face as she stood again just inside the door, listening, the glass in her hand. I'll need it later, she said. I'll need more than that. She covered the glass with a saucer and hid it carefully. Then she dug into the mass of garments in the corner and found a dancing-frock and shook it out and hung it back in the closet. She looked at the other things a moment, but she returned to the bed and lay down again. At once she rose and drew the chair up and sat down, her feet on the unmade bed. While daylight died slowly in the room she sat smoking cigarette after cigarette, listening to every sound on the stairs.

At half-past six Minnie brought her supper up. On the tray was another glass of gin. "Miss Reba sont this un," she said. "She say, how you feelin?"

"Tell her, all right," Temple said. "I'm going to have a bath and then go to bed, tell her."

undressed and in a spurious Chinese robe splotched with gold dragons and jade and scarlet flowers she left the room. When she returned her hair curled damply about her face. She went to the washstand and took up the tumbler, holding it in her hands, but she set it down again.

She dressed, retrieving the bottles and jars from the corner. Her motions before the glass were furious yet painstaking. She went to the washstand and took up the glass, but again she paused and went to the corner and got her coat and put it on and put the platinum bag in the pocket and leaned once more to the mirror. Then she went and took up the glass and gulped the gin and left the room, walking swiftly.

A single light burned in the hall. It was empty. She could hear voices in Miss Reba's room, but the lower hall was deserted. She descended swiftly and silently and gained the door. She believed that it would be at the door that they would stop her and she thought of the pistol with acute regret, almost pausing, knowing that she would use it without any compunction whatever, with a kind of pleasure. She sprang to the door and pawed at the bolt, her head turned over her shoulder.

It opened. She sprang out and out the lattice door and ran down the walk and out the gate. As she did so a car, moving slowly along the curb, stopped opposite her. Popeye sat at the wheel. Without any apparent movement from him the door swung open. He made no movement, spoke no word. He just sat there, the straw hat slanted a little aside.

passed beneath lights she could see him watching her as she struggled, tugging at his hand, whipping her head this way and that.

She ceased struggling, but she continued to twist her head from side to side, tugging at his hand. One finger, ringed with a thick ring, held her lips apart, his finger-tips digging into her cheek. With the other hand he whipped the car in and out of traffic, bearing down upon other cars until they slewed aside with brakes squealing, shooting recklessly across intersections. Once a police-man shouted at them, but he did not even look around.

Temple began to whimper, moaning behind his hand, drooling upon his fingers. The ring was like a dentist's instrument; she could not close her lips to regurgitate. When he removed it she could feel the imprint of his fingers cold on her jaw. She lifted her hand to it.

"You hurt my mouth," she whimpered. They were approaching the outskirts of the city, the speedometer at fifty miles. His hat slanted above his delicate hooked profile. She nursed her jaw. The houses gave way to broad, dark subdivisions out of which realtors' signs loomed abrupt and ghostly, with a quality of forlorn assurance. Between them low, far lights hung in the cool empty darkness blowing with fireflies. She began to cry quietly, feeling the cooling double drink of gin inside her. "You hurt my mouth," she said in a voice small and faint with self-pity. She nursed her jaw with experimental fingers, pressing harder and harder until she found a twinge. "You'll be sorry for this," she said in a muffled voice. "When I tell Red. Dont you wish you were Red?

Behind her the music beat, sultry, evocative; filled with movement of feet, the voluptuous hysteria of muscles warming the scent of flesh, of the blood. "Oh, God; oh, God," she said, her lips scarce moving. "I'll go. I'll go back."

"You took it," he said. "Go on."

In his grasp her hands made tentative plucking motions at his coat just out of reach of her finger-tips. Slowly he was turning her toward the door, her head reverted. "You just dare!" she cried. "You just—" His hand closed upon the back of her neck, his fingers like steel, yet cold and light as aluminum. She could hear the vertebrae grating faintly together, and his voice, cold and still. "Will you?"

She nodded her head. Then they were dancing. She could still feel his hand at her neck. Across his shoulder she looked swiftly about the room, her gaze flicking from face to face among the dancers. Beyond a low arch, in another room, a group stood about the crap-table. She leaned this way and that, trying to see the faces of the group.

Then she saw the four men. They were sitting at a table near the door. One of them was chewing gum; the whole lower part of his face seemed to be cropped with teeth of an unbelievable whiteness and size. When she saw them she swung Popeye around with his back to them, working the two of them toward the door again. Once more her harried gaze flew from face to face in the crowd.

When she looked again two of the men had risen. They approached. She dragged Popeye into their path, disappeared. When the music ceased she had another drink. It did no good. It merely lay hot and hard inside her. "Come on," she said, "dont quit." But he wouldn't get up, and she stood over him, her muscles flinching and jerking with exhaustion and terror. She began to jeer at him. "Call yourself a man, a bold, bad man, and let a girl dance you off your feet." Then her face drained, became small and haggard and sincere; she spoke like a child, with sober despair. "Popeye." He sat with his hands on the table, finicking with a cigarette, the second glass with its melting ice before him. She put her hand on his shoulder. "Daddy," she said. Moving to shield them from the room, her hand stole toward his armpit, touching the butt of the flat pistol. It lay rigid in the light, dead vise of his arm and side. "Give it to me," she whispered. "Daddy. Daddy." She leaned her thigh against his shoulder, caressing his arm with her flank. "Give it to me, daddy," she whispered. Suddenly her hand began to steal down his body in a swift, covert movement; then it snapped away in a movement of revulsion. "I forgot," she whispered; "I didn't mean . . . I didn't . . ."

One of the men at the other table hissed once through his teeth. "Sit down," Popeye said. She sat down. She filled her glass, watching her hands perform the action. Then she was watching the corner of the gray coat. He's got a broken button, she thought stupidly. Popeye had not moved.

"Dance this?" Red said.

His head was bent but he was not looking at her. He was turned a little, facing the two men at the other table.

ing the music without hearing the tune for a time. Then she became aware that the orchestra was playing the same tune as when Red was asking her to dance. If that were so, then it couldn't have happened yet. She felt a wild surge of relief. It was not too late: Red was still alive; she felt long shuddering waves of physical desire going over her, draining the color from her mouth, drawing her eyeballs back into her skull in a shuddering swoon.

They were at the crap-table. She could hear herself shouting to the dice. She was rolling them, winning; the counters were piling up in front of her as Popeye drew them in, coaching her, correcting her in his soft, querulous voice. He stood beside her, shorter than she.

He had the cup himself. She stood beside him cunningly, feeling the desire going over her in wave after wave, involved with the music and with the smell of her own flesh. She became quiet. By infinitesimal inches she moved aside until someone slipped into her place. Then she was walking swiftly and carefully across the floor toward the door, the dancers, the music swirling slowly about her in a bright myriad wave. The table where the two men had sat was empty, but she did not even glance at it. She entered the corridor. A waiter met her.

"Room," she said. "Hurry."

The room contained a table and four chairs. The waiter turned on the light and stood in the door. She jerked her hand at him; he went out. She leaned against the table on her braced arms, watching the door, until Red entered.

He came toward her. She did not move. Her eyes be-so that he faced the door, and slipped his right hand free. She did not seem to be aware that he had moved.

"Please. Please. Please. Please. Dont make me wait. I'm burning up."

"All right. You go on back. You wait till I give you the sign. Will you go on back?"

"I cant wait. You've got to. I'm on fire, I tell you." She clung to him. Together they blundered across the room toward the door, he holding her clear of his right side; she in a voluptuous swoon, unaware that they were moving, straining at him as though she were trying to touch him with all of her body-surface at once. He freed himself and thrust her into the passage.

"Go on," he said. "I'll be there in a minute."

"You wont be long? I'm on fire. I'm dying, I tell you."

"No. Not long. Go on, now."

The music was playing. She moved up the corridor, staggering a little. She thought that she was leaning against the wall, when she found that she was dancing again; then that she was dancing with two men at once; then she found that she was not dancing but that she was moving toward the door between the man with the chewing gum and the one with the buttoned coat. She tried to stop, but they had her under the arms; she opened her mouth to scream, taking one last despairing look about the swirling room.

"Yell," the man with the buttoned coat said. "Just try it once."

Red was at the crap-table. She saw his head turned, the cup in his lifted hand. With it he made her a short, cheery salute. He watched her disappear through the

XXV

THE TABLES had been moved to one end of the dance floor. On each one was a black table-cloth. The curtains were still drawn; a thick, salmon-colored light fell through them. Just beneath the orchestra platform the coffin sat. It was an expensive one: black, with silver fittings, the trestles hidden by a mass of flowers. In wreaths and crosses and other shapes of ceremonial mortality, the mass appeared to break in a symbolical wave over the bier and on upon the platform and the piano, the scent of them thickly oppressive.

The proprietor of the place moved about among the tables, speaking to the arrivals as they entered and found seats. The Negro waiters, in black shirts beneath their starched jackets, were already moving in and out with glasses and bottles of ginger ale. They moved with swaggering and decorous repression; already the scene was vivid, with a hushed, macabre air a little febrile.

The archway to the dice-room was draped in black.

by others with extended cups. From time to time a waiter entered with ice and fruit and dumped them into the bowl; from a suit case under the table Gene drew fresh bottles and decanted them into the bowl; then, proprietorial, adjurant, sweating, he resumed his harsh monologue, mopping his face on his sleeve. "Come on, folks. It's all on Gene. I aint nothing but a bootlegger, but he never had a better friend than me. Step up and drink, folks. There's more where that come from."

From the dance hall came a strain of music. The people entered and found seats. On the platform was the orchestra from a downtown hotel, in dinner coats. The proprietor and a second man were conferring with the leader.

"Let them play jazz," the second man said. "Never nobody liked dancing no better than Red."

"No, no," the proprietor said. "Time Gene gets them all ginned up on free whiskey, they'll start dancing. It'll look bad."

"How about the Blue Danube?" the leader said.

"No, no; dont play no blues, I tell you," the proprietor said. "There's a dead man in that bier."

"That's not blues," the leader said.

"What is it?" the second man said.

"A waltz. Strauss."

"A wop?" the second man said. "Like hell. Red was an American. You may not be, but he was. Dont you know anything American? Play I Cant Give You Anything but Love. He always liked that."

"And get them all to dancing?" the proprietor said. He glanced back at the tables, where the women were benet. Two soiled young men worked their way toward the table, shouting "Gangway. Gangway" monotonously, carrying suit cases. They opened them and set bottles on the table, while Gene, frankly weeping now, opened them and decanted them into the bowl. "Come up, folks. I couldn't a loved him no better if he'd a been my own son," he shouted hoarsely, dragging his sleeve across his face.

A waiter edged up to the table with a bowl of ice and fruit and went to put them into the punch bowl. "What the hell you doing?" Gene said, "putting that slop in there? Get to hell away from here."

"Ra-a-a-a-y-y-y-y!" they shouted, clashing their cups, drowning all save the pantomime as Gene knocked the bowl of fruit from the waiter's hand and fell again to dumping raw liquor into the bowl, sploshing it into and upon the extended hands and cups. The two youths opened bottles furiously.

As though swept there upon a brassy blare of music the proprietor appeared in the door, his face harried, waving his arms. "Come on, folks," he shouted, "let's finish the musical program. It's costing us money."

"Hell with it," they shouted.

"Costing who money?"

"Who cares?"

"Costing who money?"

"Who begrudges it? I'll pay it. By God, I'll buy him two funerals."

"Folks! Folks!" the proprietor shouted. "Dont you realise there's a bier in that room?"

bouncer. The proprietor grasped the woman as she lifted another floral piece. The man who had tried to hold her intervened, the woman cursing shrilly and striking at both of them impartially with the wreath. The bouncer caught the man's arm; he whirled and struck at the bouncer, who knocked him halfway across the room. Three more men entered. The fourth rose from the floor and all four of them rushed at the bouncer.

He felled the first and whirled and sprang with unbelievable celerity, into the main room. The orchestra was playing. It was immediately drowned in a sudden pandemonium of chairs and screams. The bouncer whirled again and met the rush of the four men. They mingled; a second man flew out and skittered along the floor on his back; the bouncer sprang free. Then he whirled and rushed them and in a whirling plunge they bore down upon the bier and crashed into it. The orchestra had ceased and were now climbing onto their chairs, with their instruments. The floral offerings flew; the coffin teetered. "Catch it!" a voice shouted. They sprang forward, but the coffin crashed heavily to the floor, coming open. The corpse tumbled slowly and sedately out and came to rest with its face in the center of a wreath.

"Play something!" the proprietor bawled, waving his arms. "Play! Play!"

When they raised the corpse the wreath came too, attached to him by a hidden end of a wire driven into his cheek. He had worn a cap which, tumbled off, exposed a small blue hole in the center of his forehead. It had been neatly plugged with wax and was painted, but the wax had been jarred out and lost. They couldn't find it, but nie opened the door they surged about Miss Reba's feet. She kicked them aside. Again they assailed her with snapping eagerness; again she flung them back against the wall in muted thuds.

"Come in, come in," she said, her hand to her breast. Once inside the house the woman with the handkerchief began to weep aloud.

"Didn't he look sweet?" she wailed. "Didn't he look sweet!"

"Now, now," Miss Reba said, leading the way to her room, "come in and have some beer. You'll feel better. Minnie!" They entered the room with the decorated dresser, the safe, the screen, the draped portrait. "Sit down, sit down," she panted, shoving the chairs forward. She lowered herself into one and stooped terrifically toward her feet.

"Uncle Bud, honey," the weeping woman said, dabbing at her eyes, "come and unlace Miss Reba's shoes."

The boy knelt and removed Miss Reba's shoes. "And if you'll just reach me them house slippers under the bed there, honey," Miss Reba said. The boy fetched the slippers. Minnie entered, followed by the dogs. They rushed at Miss Reba and began to worry the shoes she had just removed.

"Scat!" the boy said, striking at one of them with his hand. The dog's head snapped around, its teeth clicking, its half-hidden eyes bright and malevolent. The boy recoiled. "You bite me, you thon bitch," he said.

"Uncle Bud!" the fat woman said, her round face, rigid in fatty folds and streaked with tears, turned upon the boy in shocked surprise, the plumes nodding precari-

"Yes," Miss Myrtle said. "Is them two nice young fellows still with you, Miss Reba?"

"Yes," Miss Reba said. "I think I got to get shut of them, though. I aint specially tender-hearted, but after all it aint no use in helping young folks to learn this world's meanness until they have to. I already had to stop the girls running around the house without no clothes on, and they dont like it."

They drank again, decorously, handling the tankards delicately, save Miss Reba, who grasped hers as though it were a weapon, her other hand lost in her breast. She set her tankard down empty. "I get so dry, seems like," she said. "Wont you ladies have another?" They murmured, ceremoniously. "Minnie!" Miss Reba shouted.

Minnie came and filled the tankards again. "Reely, I'm right ashamed," Miss Myrtle said. "But Miss Reba has such good beer. And then we've all had a kind of upsetting afternoon."

"I'm just surprised it wasn't upset no more," Miss Reba said. "Giving away all that free liquor like Gene done."

"It must have cost a good piece of jack," the thin woman said.

"I believe you," Miss Reba said. "And who got anything out of it? Tell me that. Except the privilege of having his place hell-full of folks not spending a cent." She had set her tankard on the table beside her chair. Suddenly she turned her head sharply and looked at it. Uncle Bud was now behind her chair, leaning against the table. "You aint been into my beer, have you, boy?" she said.

"You, Uncle Bud," Miss Myrtle said. "Aint you

when we left here I was so mortified I didn't know what
to do. I was ashamed to be seen on the street with a drunk
boy like you."

Miss Reba emerged from behind the screen with three
glasses of gin. "This'll put some heart into us," she said.
"We're setting here like three old sick cats." They bowed
formally and drank, patting their lips. Then they began
to talk. They were all talking at once, again in half-com-
pleted sentences, but without pauses for agreement or
affirmation.

"It's us girls," Miss Myrtle said. "Men just cant seem to
take us and leave us for what we are. They make us what
we are, then they expect us to be different. Expect us not
to never look at another man, while they come and go as
they please."

"A woman that wants to fool with more than one man
at a time is a fool," Miss Reba said. "They're all trouble,
and why do you want to double your trouble? And the
woman that cant stay true to a good man when she gets
him, a free-hearted spender that never give her a hour's
uneasiness or a hard word . . ." looking at them, her eyes
began to fill with a sad, unutterable expression, of baffled
and patient despair.

"Now, now," Miss Myrtle said. She leaned forward and
patted Miss Reba's huge hand. Miss Lorraine made
a faint clucking sound with her tongue. "You'll get yourself started."

"He was such a good man," Miss Reba said. "We was
like two doves. For twenty-five years we was like two
doves."

something funny about him. There's a funny business somewhere."

"He was a free spender, all right," Miss Lorraine said.

"The clothes and jewelry that girl bought, it was a shame," Miss Reba said. "There was a Chinee robe she paid a hundred dollars for—imported, it was—and perfume at ten dollars an ounce; next morning when I went up there, they was all wadded in the corner and the perfume and rouge busted all over them like a cyclone. That's what she'd do when she got mad at him, when he'd beat her. After he shut her up and wouldn't let her leave the house. Having the front of my house watched like it was a . . ." She raised the tankard from the table to her lips. Then she halted it, blinking. "Where's my—"

"Uncle Bud!" Miss Myrtle said. She grasped the boy by the arm and snatched him out from behind Miss Reba's chair and shook him, his round head bobbing on his shoulders with an expression of equable idiocy. "Aint you ashamed? Aint you *ashamed?* Why cant you stay out of these ladies' beer? I'm a good mind to take that dollar back and make you buy Miss Reba a can of beer, I am for a fact. Now, you go over there by that window and stay there, you hear?"

"Nonsense," Miss Reba said. "There wasn't much left. You ladies are about ready too, aint you? Minnie!"

Miss Lorraine touched her mouth with her handkerchief. Behind her glasses her eyes rolled aside in a veiled, secret look. She laid the other hand to her flat spinster's breast.

"We forgot about your heart, honey," Miss Myrtle

"Uncle Bud, honey," Miss Myrtle said, "dont you want to go and play in the yard with Reba and Mr Binford?"

"Yessum," the boy said. He went toward the door. They watched him until the door closed upon him. Miss Lorraine drew her chair up; they leaned together.

"And that's what they was doing?" Miss Myrtle said.

"I says 'I been running a house for thirty years, but this is the first time I ever had anything like this going on in it. If you want to turn a stud in to your girl' I says 'go somewhere else to do it. I aint going to have my house turned into no French joint.'"

"The son of a bitch," Miss Lorraine said.

"He'd ought to've had sense enough to got a old ugly man," Miss Myrtle said. "Tempting us poor girls like that."

"Men always expects us to resist temptation," Miss Lorraine said. She was sitting upright like a school-teacher. "The lousy son of a bitch."

"Except what they offers themselves," Miss Reba said. "Then watch them. . . . Every morning for four days that was going on, then they didn't come back. For a week Popeye didn't show up at all, and that girl wild as a young mare. I thought he was out of town on business maybe, until Minnie told me he wasn't and that he give her five dollars a day not to let that girl out of the house nor use the telephone. And me trying to get word to him to come and take her out of my house because I didn't want nuttin like that going on in it. Yes, sir, Minnie said the two of them would be nekkid as two snakes, and Popeye hanging over the foot of the bed without even his hat off, making a kind of whinnying sound."

XXVi

WHEN THE SUN rose, Horace had not been to bed nor even undressed. He was just finishing a letter to his wife, addressed to her at her father's in Kentucky, asking for a divorce. He sat at the table, looking down at the single page written neatly and illegibly over, feeling quiet and empty for the first time since he had found Popeye watching him across the spring four weeks ago. While he was sitting there he began to smell coffee from somewhere. "I'll finish this business and then I'll go to Europe. I am sick. I am too old for this. I was born too old for it, and so I am sick to death for quiet."

He shaved and made coffee and drank a cup and ate some bread. When he passed the hotel, the bus which met the morning train was at the curb, with the drummers getting into it. Clarence Snopes was one of them, carrying a tan suit case.

"Going down to Jackson for a couple of days on a little business," he said. "Too bad I missed you last night. I he resigned from his job in the commons; he also had a new suit. People were glad that he had saved through his industry to where he could give all his time to his studies. He was in the law school then, and the law professors groomed him like a race-horse. He graduated well, though without distinction. "Because he was handicapped at the start," the professors said. "If he had had the same start that the others had . . . He will go far," they said.

It was not until he had left school that they learned that he had been playing poker for three years in the office of a livery stable, behind drawn shades. When, two years out of school, he got elected to the State legislature, they began to tell an anecdote of his school days.

It was in the poker game in the livery stable office. The bet came to Graham. He looked across the table at the owner of the stable, who was his only remaining opponent.

"How much have you got there, Mr Harris?" he said.

"Forty-two dollars, Eustace," the proprietor said. Eustace shoved some chips into the pot. "How much is that?" the proprietor said.

"Forty-two dollars, Mr Harris."

"Hmmm," the proprietor said. He examined his hand. "How many cards did you draw, Eustace?"

"Three, Mr Harris."

"Hmmm. Who dealt the cards, Eustace?"

"I did, Mr Harris."

"I pass, Eustace."

He had been District Attorney but a short time, yet already he had let it be known that he would announce

sons for wanting Horace out of this case. The sooner the
better. Three nights ago that Snopes, the one in the legislature, telephoned out home, trying to find him. The
next day he went to Memphis. I dont know what for.
You'll have to find that out yourself. I just want Horace
out of this business as soon as possible."

She rose and moved toward the door. He hobbled over
to open it; again she put that cold, still, unfathomable
gaze upon him as though he were a dog or a cow and she
waited for it to get out of her path. Then she was gone.
He closed the door and struck a clumsy clog-step, snapping his fingers just as the door opened again; he
snapped his hands toward his tie and looked at her in
the door, holding it open.

"What day do you think it will be over with?" she said.

"Why, I cuh— Court opens the twentieth," he said. "It
will be the first case. Say . . . Two days. Or three at the
most, with your kind assistance. And I need not assure
you that this will be held in strictest confidence between
us. . . ." He moved toward her, but her blank calculating gaze was like a wall, surrounding him.

"That will be the twenty-fourth." Then she was looking at him again. "Thank you," she said, and closed the
door.

That night she wrote Belle that Horace would be home
on the twenty-fourth. She telephoned Horace and asked
for Belle's address.

"Why?" Horace said.

"I'm going to write her a letter," she said, her
voice tranquil, without threat. Dammit, Horace thought,
holding the dead wire in his hand, How can I be ex-

ten times as much for the same thing than the lowlife jew, we need a law. I been a liberal spender all my life; whatever I had has always been my friends' too. But when a durn, stinking, lowlife jew will refuse to pay an American one tenth of what another American, and a judge at that—"

"Why did you sell it to him, then?" the barber said.

"What?" Snopes said. The barber was looking at him.

"What was you trying to sell to that car when it run over you?" the barber said.

"Have a cigar," Snopes said.

we got started crying too. Me and Minnie and Miss Myrtle. We drunk up a whole new bottle of gin. I cant afford
that. So dont you be sending no jay cops up here with no
letters for nobody. You telephone me and I'll turn them
both out on the street and you can have them arrested
there."

On the night of the nineteenth he telephoned her
again. He had some trouble in getting in touch with her.

"They're gone," she said. "Both of them. Dont you read
no papers?"

"What papers?" Horace said. "Hello. Hello!"

"They aint here no more, I said," Miss Reba said. "I
dont know nuttin about them and I dont want to know
nuttin except who's going to pay me a week's room rent
on—"

"But cant you find where she went to? I may need her."

"I dont know nuttin and I dont want to know nuttin,"
Miss Reba said. He heard the receiver click. Yet the dis-
connection was not made at once. He heard the receiver
thud onto the table where the telephone sat, and he
could hear Miss Reba shouting for Minnie: "Minnie. Minnie!" Then some hand lifted the receiver and set it onto
the hook; the wire clicked in his ear. After a while a detached Delsarte-ish voice said: "Pine Bluff dizzent . . .
Enkyew!"

The trial opened the next day. On the table lay the
sparse objects which the District Attorney was offering:
the bullet from Tommy's skull, a stoneware jug contain-
ing corn whiskey.

"I will call Mrs Goodwin to the stand," Horace said.

is won? That they are reduced to trying to impugn the character of your witness?" But when they left the jail he found the woman still watching him from some deep reserve of foreboding. "You mustn't worry at all, I tell you. You may know more about making whiskey or love than I do, but I know more about criminal procedure than you, remember."

"You dont think I made a mistake?"

"I know you didn't. Dont you see how that explodes their case? The best they can hope for now is a hung jury. And the chances of that are not one in fifty. I tell you, he'll walk out of that jail tomorrow a free man."

"Then I guess it's time to think about paying you."

"Yes," Horace said, "all right. I'll come out tonight."

"Tonight?"

"Yes. He may call you back to the stand tomorrow. We'd better prepare for it, anyway."

At eight oclock he entered the mad woman's yard. A single light burned in the crazy depths of the house, like a firefly caught in a brier patch, but the woman did not appear when he called. He went to the door and knocked. A shrill voice shouted something; he waited a moment. He was about to knock again when he heard the voice again, shrill and wild and faint, as though from a distance, like a reedy pipe buried by an avalanche. He circled the house in the rank, waist-high weeds. The kitchen door was open. The lamp was there, dim in a smutty chimney, filling the room—a jumble of looming shapes rank with old foul female flesh—not with light but with shadow. White eyeballs rolled in a high, tight bullet head in brown gleams above a torn singlet strapped into good man. If you'll just promise to get the kid a newspaper grift when he's old enough to make change, I'll be easy in my mind."

The woman had returned to the cot. She lifted the child onto her lap. Horace went to her. He said: "You come on, now. Nothing's going to happen. He'll be all right here. He knows it. You've got to go home and get some sleep, because you'll both be leaving here tomorrow. Come, now."

"I reckon I better stay," she said.

"Damn it, dont you know that putting yourself in the position for disaster is the surest way in the world to bring it about? Hasn't your own experience shown you that? Lee knows it. Lee, make her stop this."

"Go on, Ruby," Goodwin said. "Go home and go to bed."

"I reckon I better stay," she said.

Horace stood over them. The woman mused above the child, her face bent and her whole body motionless. Goodwin leaned back against the wall, his brown wrists folded into the faded sleeves of his shirt. "You're a man now," Horace said. "Aren't you? I wish that jury could see you now, locked up in a concrete cell, scaring women and children with fifth grade ghost stories. They'd know you never had the guts to kill anybody."

"You better go on and go to bed yourself," Goodwin said. "We could sleep here, if there wasn't so much noise going on."

"No; that's too sensible for us to do," Horace said. He left the cell. The jailer unlocked the door for him and he quitted the building. In ten minutes he returned, with a

"Shall we lay him down?" Horace whispered.

"No. Let him stay there." Moving quietly she laid the child on the cot and moved herself to the other end of it. Horace carried the chair over beside her. They spoke in whispers.

The clock struck eleven. Still Horace drilled her, going over and over the imaginary scene. At last he said: "I think that's all. Can you remember it, now? If he should ask you anything you cant answer in the exact words you've learned tonight, just say nothing for a moment. I'll attend to the rest. Can you remember, now?"

"Yes," she whispered. He reached across and took the box of candy from the cot and opened it, the glazed paper crackling faintly. She took a piece. Goodwin had not moved. She looked at him, then at the narrow slit of window.

"Stop that," Horace whispered. "He couldn't reach him through that window with a hat-pin, let alone a bullet. Dont you know that?"

"Yes," she said. She held the bon-bon in her hand. She was not looking at him. "I know what you're thinking," she whispered.

"What?"

"When you got to the house and I wasn't there. I know what you're thinking." Horace watched her, her averted face. "You said tonight was the time to start paying you."

For a while longer he looked at her. "Ah," he said. "O tempora! O mores! O hell! Can you stupid mammals never believe that any man, every man— You thought that was what I was coming for? You thought that if I had intended to, I'd have waited this long?"

dropped it behind the cot. Horace extended his handker-chief.

"It'll soil it," she said. "Wait." She wiped her fingers on the child's discarded garment and sat again, her hands clasped in her lap. Goodwin was snoring regularly. "When he went to the Philippines he left me in San Fran-cisco. I got a job and I lived in a hall room, cooking over a gas-jet, because I told him I would. I didn't know how long he'd be gone, but I promised him I would and he knew I would. When he killed that other soldier over that nigger woman, I didn't even know it. I didn't get a letter from him for five months. It was just when I happened to see an old newspaper I was spreading on a closet shelf in the place where I worked that I saw the regiment was coming home, and when I looked at the calendar it was that day. I'd been good all that time. I'd had good chances; every day I had them with the men coming in the restaurant.

"They wouldn't let me off to go and meet the ship, so I had to quit. Then they wouldn't let me see him, wouldn't even let me on the ship. I stood there while they came marching off it, watching for him and asking the ones that passed if they knew where he was and them kidding me if I had a date that night, telling me they never heard of him or that he was dead or he had run off to Japan with the colonel's wife. I tried to get on the ship again, but they wouldn't let me. So that night I dressed up and went to the cabarets until I found one of them and let him pick me up, and he told me. It was like I had died. I sat there with the music playing and all, and that drunk soldier pawing at me, and me wondering why I she looked at Horace, turning upon him a blank, musing gaze for an unhurried moment. Through the slotted window the darkness came chill and dead.

Goodwin ceased snoring. He stirred and sat up.

"What time is it?" he said.

"What?" Horace said. He looked at his watch. "Half-past two."

"He must have had a puncture," Goodwin said.

Toward dawn Horace himself slept, sitting in the chair. When he waked a narrow rosy pencil of sunlight fell level through the window. Goodwin and the woman were talking quietly on the cot. Goodwin looked at him bleakly.

"Morning," he said.

"I hope you slept off that nightmare of yours," Horace said.

"If I did, it's the last one I'll have. They say you dont dream there."

"You've certainly done enough not to miss it," Horace said. "I suppose you'll believe us, after this."

"Believe, hell," Goodwin said, who had sat so quiet, so contained, with his saturnine face, negligent in his overalls and blue shirt; "do you think for one minute that man is going to let me walk out of that door and up the street and into that courthouse, after yesterday? What sort of men have you lived with all your life? In a nursery? I wouldn't do that, myself."

"If he does, he has sprung his own trap," Horace said.

"What good will that do me? Let me tell—"

"Lee," the woman said.

—"you something: the next time you want to play dice with a man's neck—"

you have lived. So you see that folly, as well as poverty, cares for its own."

"And you know that he—that—"

"Stop it, now. We dreamed that away, too. God is foolish at times, but at least He's a gentleman. Dont you know that?"

"I always thought of Him as a man," the woman said.

The bell was already ringing when Horace crossed the square toward the courthouse. Already the square was filled with wagons and cars and the overalls and khaki thronged slowly beneath the gothic entrance of the building. Overhead the clock was striking nine as he mounted the stairs.

The broad double doors at the head of the cramped stair were open. From beyond them came a steady preliminary stir of people settling themselves. Above the seat-backs Horace could see their heads—bald heads, gray heads, shaggy heads and heads trimmed to recent feather-edge above sun-baked necks, oiled heads above urban collars and here and there a sunbonnet or a flowered hat.

The hum of their voices and movements came back upon the steady draft which blew through the door. The air entered the open windows and blew over the heads and back to Horace in the door, laden with smells of tobacco and stale sweat and the earth and with that unmistakable odor of courtrooms; that musty odor of spent lusts and greeds and bickerings and bitterness, and withal a certain clumsy stability in lieu of anything bet-

Horace realised that he was being spoken to, a little tes-
tily, by the Court.

"Is this your witness, Mr Benbow?"

"It is, your Honor."

"You wish her sworn and recorded?"

"I do, your Honor."

Beyond the window, beneath the unhurried pigeons,
the bailiff's voice still droned, reiterant, importunate, and
detached, though the sound of the bell had ceased.

the jury to disregard it, Mr Benbow. Keep to the matter in hand, Mr District Attorney."

The District Attorney bowed. He turned to the witness stand, where Temple sat. From beneath her black hat her hair escaped in tight red curls like clots of resin. The hat bore a rhinestone ornament. Upon her black satin lap lay a platinum bag. Her pale tan coat was open upon a shoulder knot of purple. Her hands lay motionless, palm-up on her lap. Her long blonde legs slanted, lax-ankled, her two motionless slippers with their glittering buckles lay on their sides as though empty. Above the ranked intent faces white and pallid as the floating bellies of dead fish, she sat in an attitude at once detached and cringing, her gaze fixed on something at the back of the room. Her face was quite pale, the two spots of rouge like paper discs pasted on her cheek bones, her mouth painted into a savage and perfect bow, also like something both symbolical and cryptic cut carefully from purple paper and pasted there.

The District Attorney stood before her.

"What is your name?" She did not answer. She moved her head slightly, as though he had obstructed her view, gazing at something in the back of the room. "What is your name?" he repeated, moving also, into the line of her vision again. Her mouth moved. "Louder," he said. "Speak out. No one will hurt you. Let these good men, these fathers and husbands, hear what you have to say and right your wrong for you."

The Court glanced at Horace, his eyebrows raised. But Horace made no move. He sat with his head bent a little, his hands clutched in his lap.

"You were in hiding, then, because something had happened to you and you dared not—"

"I object!" Horace said. "The question is lead—"

"Sustained," the Court said. "I have been on the point
of warning you for some time, Mr Attorney, but defendant would not take exception, for some reason."

The District Attorney bowed toward the Bench. He
turned to the witness and held her eyes again.

"Where were you on Sunday morning, May twelfth?"

"I was in the crib."

The room sighed, its collective breath hissing in the
musty silence. Some newcomers entered, but they
stopped at the rear of the room in a clump and stood
there. Temple's head had moved again. The District Attorney caught her gaze and held it. He half turned and
pointed at Goodwin.

"Did you ever see that man before?" She gazed at the
District Attorney, her face quite rigid, empty. From a
short distance her eyes, the two spots of rouge and her
mouth, were like five meaningless objects in a small
heart-shaped dish. "Look where I am pointing."

"Yes."

"Where did you see him?"

"In the crib."

"What were you doing in the crib?"

"I was hiding."

"Who were you hiding from?"

"From him."

"That man there? Look where I am pointing."

"Yes."

believable, story which this young girl has told; you have seen the evidence and heard the doctor's testimony: I shall no longer subject this ruined, defenseless child to the agony of—" he ceased; the heads turned as one and watched a man come stalking up the aisle toward the Bench. He walked steadily, paced and followed by a slow gaping of the small white faces, a slow hissing of collars. He had neat white hair and a clipped moustache like a bar of hammered silver against his dark skin. His eyes were pouched a little. A small paunch was buttoned snugly into his immaculate linen suit. He carried a panama hat in one hand and a slender black stick in the other. He walked steadily up the aisle in a slow expulsion of silence like a prolonged sigh, looking to neither side. He passed the witness stand without a glance at the witness, who still gazed at something in the back of the room, walking right through her line of vision like a runner crossing a tape, and stopped before the bar above which the Court had half-risen, his arms on the desk.

"Your Honor," the old man said, "is the Court done with this witness?"

"Yes, sir, Judge," the Court said; "yes, sir. Defendant, do you waive—"

The old man turned slowly, erect above the held breaths, the little white faces, and looked down at the six people at the counsel table. Behind him the witness had not moved. She sat in her attitude of childish immobility, gazing like a drugged person above the faces, toward the rear of the room. The old man turned to her and extended his hand. She did not move. The room expelled its breath, sucked it quickly in and held it again.

and the woman with the child and Horace and the District Attorney and the Memphis lawyer sat, and across the jury and against the Bench in a long sigh. The Memphis lawyer was sitting on his spine, gazing dreamily out the window. The child made a fretful sound, whimpering.

"Hush," the woman said. "Shhhhhhhh."

the courthouse. Beside the gate the woman stood, in the gray hat with the veil, carrying the child in her arms. "Standing where he can see it through the window," Horace said. "I smell ham, too. Maybe he'll be eating ham before we get home." Then he began to cry, sitting in the car beside his sister. She drove steadily, not fast. Soon they had left the town and the stout rows of young cotton swung at either hand in parallel and diminishing retrograde. There was still a little snow of locust blooms on the mounting drive. "It does last," Horace said. "Spring does. You'd almost think there was some purpose to it."

He stayed to supper. He ate a lot. "I'll go and see about your room," his sister said, quite gently.

"All right," Horace said. "It's nice of you." She went out. Miss Jenny's wheel chair sat on a platform slotted for the wheels. "It's nice of her," Horace said. "I think I'll go outside and smoke my pipe."

"Since when have you quit smoking it in here?" Miss Jenny said.

"Yes," Horace said. "It was nice of her." He walked across the porch. "I intended to stop here," Horace said. He watched himself cross the porch and then tread the diffident snow of the last locusts; he turned out of the iron gates, onto the gravel. After about a mile a car slowed and offered him a ride. "I'm just walking before supper," he said; "I'll turn back soon." After another mile he could see the lights of town. It was a faint glare, low and close. It got stronger as he approached. Before he reached town he began to hear the sound, the voices. Then he saw the people, a shifting mass filling the street,

"He wouldn't a never got a trial, in my town," a second said.

"To jail, even," a third said. "Who was she?"

"College girl. Good looker. Didn't you see her?"

"I saw her. She was some baby. Jeez. I wouldn't have used no cob."

Then the square was quiet. The clock struck eleven; the drummers went in and the Negro porter came and turned the chairs back into the wall. "You waiting for the train?" he said to Horace.

"Yes. Have you got a report on it yet?"

"It's on time. But that's two hours yet. You could lay down in the Sample Room, if you want."

"Can I?" Horace said.

"I'll show you," the Negro said. The Sample Room was where the drummers showed their wares. It contained a sofa. Horace turned off the light and lay down on the sofa. He could see the trees about the courthouse, and one wing of the building rising above the quiet and empty square. But people were not asleep. He could feel the wakefulness, the people awake about the town. "I could not have gone to sleep, anyway," he said to himself.

He heard the clock strike twelve. Then—it might have been thirty minutes or maybe longer than that—he heard someone pass under the window, running. The runner's feet sounded louder than a horse, echoing across the empty square, the peaceful hours given to sleeping. It was not a sound Horace heard now; it was something in the air which the sound of the running feet died into.

When he went down the corridor toward the stairs he did not know he was running until he heard beyond a now indistinguishable, the flames whirling in long and thunderous plumes from a white-hot mass out of which there defined themselves faintly the ends of a few posts and planks. Horace ran among them; they were holding him, but he did not know it; they were talking, but he could not hear the voices.

"It's his lawyer."

"Here's the man that defended him. That tried to get him clear."

"Put him in, too. There's enough left to burn a lawyer."

"Do to the lawyer what we did to him. What he did to her. Only we never used a cob. We made him wish we had used a cob."

Horace couldn't hear them. He couldn't hear the man who had got burned screaming. He couldn't hear the fire, though it still swirled upward unabated, as though it were living upon itself, and soundless: a voice of fury like in a dream, roaring silently out of a peaceful void.

"Late?" Horace said.

"She got in this morning. I took her home. Your wife."

"Oh," Horace said. "She's home?"

The other started the car and backed and turned. It was a good, powerful car, moving easily. "When did you expect her? . . ." They went on. "I see where they burned that fellow over at Jefferson. I guess you saw it."

"Yes," Horace said. "Yes. I heard about it."

"Served him right," the driver said. "We got to protect our girls. Might need them ourselves."

They turned, following a street. There was a corner, beneath an arc light. "I'll get out here," Horace said.

"I'll take you on to the door," the driver said.

"I'll get out here," Horace said. "Save you having to turn."

"Suit yourself," the driver said. "You're paying for it, anyway."

Horace got out and lifted out his suit case; the driver did not offer to touch it. The car went on. Horace picked up the suit case, the one which had stayed in the closet at his sister's home for ten years and which he had brought into town with him on the morning when she had asked him the name of the District Attorney.

His house was new, on a fairish piece of lawn, the trees, the poplars and maples which he had set out, still new. Before he reached the house, he saw the rose-colored shade at his wife's windows. He entered the house from the back and came to her door and looked into the room. She was reading in bed, a broad magazine with a colsomething out of a book he had read: "Less oft is peace. Less oft is peace," he said.

The wire answered. "Hello! Hello! Belle?" Horace said.

"Yes?" her voice came back thin and faint. "What is it? Is anything wrong?"

"No, no," Horace said. "I just wanted to tell you hello and good night."

"Tell what? What is it? Who is speaking?" Horace held the receiver, sitting in the dark hall.

"It's me, Horace. Horace. I just wanted to—"

Over the thin wire there came a scuffling sound; he could hear Little Belle breathe. Then a voice said, a masculine voice: "Hello, Horace; I want you to meet a—"

"Hush!" Little Belle's voice said, thin and faint; again Horace heard them scuffling; a breathless interval. "Stop it!" Little Belle's voice said. "It's Horace! I live with him!" Horace held the receiver to his ear. Little Belle's voice was breathless, controlled, cool, discreet, detached. "Hello. Horace. Is Mamma all right?"

"Yes. We're all right. I just wanted to tell you . . ."

"Oh. Good night."

"Good night. Are you having a good time?"

"Yes. Yes. I'll write tomorrow. Didn't Mamma get my letter today?"

"I dont know. I just—"

"Maybe I forgot to mail it. I wont forget tomorrow, though. I'll write tomorrow. Was that all you wanted?"

"Yes. Just wanted to tell you . . ."

He put the receiver back; he heard the wire die. The light from his wife's room fell across the hall. "Lock the back door," she said.

"By who?" the strike-breaker said. They walked along together. He was well-dressed. "Them others would take me that quick. They know it, too."

"Who would take you?"

"The strikers. I dont care a damn who is running the car, see. I'll ride with one as soon as another. Sooner, if I could make this route every night at this time."

She walked beside him. "You dont mean that," she said.

"Sure I do." He took her arm.

"I guess you'd just as soon be married to one as another, the same way."

"Who told you that?" he said. "Have them bastards been talking about me?"

A month later she told him that they would have to be married.

"How do you mean, have to?" he said.

"I dont dare to tell them. I would have to go away. I dont dare."

"Well, dont get upset. I'd just as lief. I have to pass here every night anyway."

They were married. He would pass the corner at night. He would ring the foot-bell. Sometimes he would come home. He would give her money. Her mother liked him: he would come roaring into the house at dinner time on Sunday, calling the other clients, even the old ones, by their first names. Then one day he didn't come back; he didn't ring the foot-bell when the trolley passed. The strike was over by then. She had a Christmas card from him; a picture, with a bell and an embossed wreath in gilt, from a Georgia town. It said: "The boys trying to said. "They set the house on fire." The next day, all the clients left.

The young woman quit her job. She stayed at home all the time. "You ought to get out and get some air," the grandmother said.

"I get enough air," the daughter said.

"You could go out and buy the groceries," the mother said. "You could buy them cheaper."

"We get them cheap enough."

She would watch all the fires; she would not have a match in the house. She kept a few hidden behind a brick in the outside wall. Popeye was three years old then. He looked about one, though he could eat pretty well. A doctor had told his mother to feed him eggs cooked in olive oil. One afternoon the grocer's boy, entering the area-way on a bicycle, skidded and fell. Something leaked from the package. "It aint eggs," the boy said. "See?" It was a bottle of olive oil. "You ought to buy that oil in cans, anyway," the boy said. "He cant tell no difference in it. I'll bring you another one. And you want to have that gate fixed. Do you want I should break my neck on it?"

He had not returned by six oclock. It was summer. There was no fire, not a match in the house. "I'll be back in five minutes," the daughter said.

She left the house. The grandmother watched her disappear. Then she wrapped the child up in a light blanket and left the house. The street was a side street, just off a main street where there were markets, where the rich people in limousines stopped on the way home to shop.

The policeman dug into his pocket. "Why didn't you buy some while you were there?" he said.

"I just forgot it. You know how it is, shopping with a child."

"Where is the child?" the policeman said.

"I traded it in," the woman said.

"You ought to be in vaudeville," the policeman said. "How many matches do you want? I aint got but one or two."

"Just one," the woman said. "I never do light a fire with but one."

"You ought to be in vaudeville," the policeman said. "You'd bring down the house."

"I am," the woman said. "I bring down the house."

"What house?" He looked at her. "The poor house?"

"I'll bring it down," the woman said. "You watch the papers tomorrow. I hope they get my name right."

"What's your name? Calvin Coolidge?"

"No, sir. That's my boy."

"Oh. That's why you had so much trouble shopping, is it? You ought to be in vaudeville. . . . Will two matches be enough?"

They had had three alarms from that address, so they didn't hurry. The first to arrive was the daughter. The door was locked and when the firemen came and chopped it down, the house was already gutted. The grandmother was leaning out an upstairs window through which the smoke already curled. "Them bastards," she said. "They thought they would get him. But I told them I would show them. I told them so."

The mother thought that Popeye had perished also.

be found. Finally a servant found a bathroom door locked. They called the child, but got no answer. They sent for a locksmith, but in the meantime the woman, frightened, had the door broken in with an axe. The bathroom was empty. The window was open. It gave onto a lower roof, from which a drain-pipe descended to the ground. But Popeye was gone. On the floor lay a wicker cage in which two lovebirds lived; beside it lay the birds themselves, and the bloody scissors with which he had cut them up alive.

Three months later, at the instigation of a neighbor of his mother, Popeye was arrested and sent to a home for incorrigible children. He had cut up a half-grown kitten the same way.

His mother was an invalid. The woman who had tried to befriend the child supported her, letting her do needlework and such. After Popeye was out—he was let out after five years, his behavior having been impeccable, as being cured—he would write to her two or three times a year, from Mobile and then New Orleans and then Memphis. Each summer he would return home to see her, prosperous, quiet, thin, black, and uncommunicative in his narrow black suits. He told her that his business was being night clerk in hotels; that, following his profession, he would move from town to town, as a doctor or a lawyer might.

While he was on his way home that summer they arrested him for killing a man in one town and at an hour when he was in another town killing somebody else— that man who made money and had nothing he could do with it, spend it for, since he knew that alcohol would

"You'd better get your lawyer," the judge said.

"All right," Popeye said. He turned and spoke generally into the room: "Any of you ginneys want a one-day job?"

The judge rapped on the table. Popeye turned back, his tight shoulders lifted in a faint shrug, his hand moving toward the pocket where he carried his cigarettes. The judge appointed him counsel, a young man just out of law school.

"And I wont bother about being sprung," Popeye said. "Get it over with all at once."

"You wouldn't get any bail from me, anyway," the judge told him.

"Yeuh?" Popeye said. "All right, Jack," he told his lawyer, "get going. I'm due in Pensacola right now."

"Take the prisoner back to jail," the judge said.

His lawyer had an ugly, eager, earnest face. He rattled on with a kind of gaunt enthusiasm while Popeye lay on the cot, smoking, his hat over his eyes, motionless as a basking snake save for the periodical movement of the hand that held the cigarette. At last he said: "Here. I aint the judge. Tell him all this."

"But I've got—"

"Sure. Tell it to them. I dont know nothing about it. I wasn't even there. Get out and walk it off."

The trial lasted one day. While a fellow policeman, a cigar-clerk, a telephone girl testified, while his own lawyer rebutted in a gaunt mixture of uncouth enthusiasm and earnest ill-judgment, Popeye lounged in his chair, looking out the window above the jury's heads. Now and then he yawned; his hand moved to the pocket where his

"Dont forget that lotion," Popeye said. "Ed Pinaud." He called it "Py-nawd."

It had been a gray summer, a little cool. Little daylight ever reached the cell, and a light burned in the corridor all the time, falling into the cell in a broad pale mosaic, reaching the cot where his feet lay. The turnkey gave him a chair. He used it for a table; upon it the dollar watch lay, and a carton of cigarettes and a cracked soup bowl of stubs, and he lay on the cot, smoking and contemplating his feet while day after day passed. The gleam of his shoes grew duller, and his clothes needed pressing, because he lay in them all the time, since it was cool in the stone cell.

One day the turnkey said: "There's folks here says that deppity invited killing. He done two-three mean things folks knows about." Popeye smoked, his hat over his face. The turnkey said: "They might not sent your telegram. You want me to send another one for you?" Leaning against the grating he could see Popeye's feet, his thin, black legs motionless, merging into the delicate bulk of his prone body and the hat slanted across his averted face, the cigarette in one small hand. His feet were in shadow, in the shadow of the turnkey's body where it blotted out the grating. After a while the turnkey went away quietly.

When he had six days left the turnkey offered to bring him magazines, a deck of cards.

"What for?" Popeye said. For the first time he looked at the turnkey, his head lifted, in his smooth, pallid face his eyes round and soft as those prehensile tips on a child's toy arrows. Then he lay back again. After that behind him, where he had heard Popeye moving and saw twelve marks at spaced intervals along the base of the wall, as though marked there with burned matches. Two of the spaces were filled with cigarette stubs laid in neat rows. In the third space were two stubs. Before he departed he watched Popeye rise and go there and crush out two more stubs and lay them carefully beside the others.

Just after five oclock the minister returned. All the spaces were filled save the twelfth one. It was three quarters complete. Popeye was lying on the cot. "Ready to go?" he said.

"Not yet," the minister said. "Try to pray," he said. "Try."

"Sure," Popeye said; "go ahead." The minister knelt again. He heard Popeye rise once and cross the floor and then return.

At five-thirty the turnkey came. "I brought—" he said. He held his closed fist dumbly through the grating. "Here's your change from that hundred you never— I brought . . . It's forty-eight dollars," he said. "Wait; I'll count it again; I dont know exactly, but I can give you a list—them tickets . . ."

"Keep it," Popeye said, without moving. "Buy yourself a hoop."

They came for him at six. The minister went with him, his hand under Popeye's elbow, and he stood beneath the scaffold praying, while they adjusted the rope, dragging it over Popeye's sleek, oiled head, breaking his hair loose. His hands were tied, so he began to jerk his head, coating of tortured Tschaikovsky on a slice of stale bread, while the twilight dissolved in wet gleams from the branches, onto the pavilion and the sombre toad-stools of umbrellas. Rich and resonant the brasses crashed and died in the thick green twilight, rolling over them in rich sad waves. Temple yawned behind her hand, then she took out a compact and opened it upon a face in miniature sullen and discontented and sad. Beside her her father sat, his hands crossed on the head of his stick, the rigid bar of his moustache beaded with mois-ture like frosted silver. She closed the compact and from beneath her smart new hat she seemed to follow with her eyes the waves of music, to dissolve into the dying brasses, across the pool and the opposite semicircle of trees where at sombre intervals the dead tranquil queens in stained marble mused, and on into the sky lying prone and vanquished in the embrace of the season of rain and death.

WILLIAM FAULKNER, born New Albany, Mississippi, September 25, 1897—died July 6, 1962. Attended
University of Mississippi. Enlisted Royal Air Force,
Canada, 1918. Traveled in Europe 1925-1926. Resident
of Oxford, Mississippi, where he held various jobs
while trying to establish himself as a writer. First pub-
lished novel, Soldiers' Pay, 1926. Writer in Residence
at the University of Virginia 1957-1958. Awarded the
Nobel Prize for Literature 1950.

SANCTUARY, the sixth of William Faulkner's novels
in order of publication, first appeared on February 9,
1931, but a draft of the manuscript had been finished
nearly two years earlier. The first Modern Library
edition of Sanctuary appeared in the following year
(1932), printed from the original plates, as all subse-
quent editions have been. These plates, because of the
conditions surrounding their production, had a larger
than usual number of typographical errors, most of
them immediately recognizable as such. Some were
discovered and corrected from time to time, but many
remained. A great effort has been made in this new
edition, which was entirely reset, to produce, with the
co-operation of the author, the definitive text.

VINTAGE BELLES-LETTRES